D0407149

OCT 0 1 2019

Praise for
A HOUSE OF RAGE AND SORROW

"Mandanna is an astute observer of human nature and a master of suspense. . . . Extraordinarily drawn characters and plot twists will keep readers' hearts racing."
—*Kirkus Reviews*, starred review

"A rare gem of a sequel that manages to be even better than the first book! Each page drips with action and moral complexities, and plot twists that will both make and break your heart. Perfect for readers looking for sharp, smart, fast-paced fantasies, especially with fierce female leads."
—Natasha Ngan, *New York Times* bestselling author of
Girls of Paper and Fire

"A thrilling sequel to Mandanna's incredible *A Spark of White Fire*. *A House of Rage and Sorrow* takes a gorgeously rendered world of spaceship kingdoms, meddling gods, and galaxy-shaking prophecies and pairs it perfectly with an achingly intimate family drama. I cannot wait for the conclusion!"
—S. A. Chakraborty, author of *The City of Brass*
and *The Kingdom of Copper*

Praise for
A SPARK OF WHITE FIRE

"Sangu Mandanna's *A Spark of White Fire* is full of brilliant, complex characters against a compelling mythological canvas. It's full of love and gods, reversals and surprises. I loved it and can't wait for the next book."
—Kat Howard, Alex Award-winning author of
An Unkindness of Magicians

Other mortals

SELWYN COFFYN, the former advisor to King Elvar. Also Queen Guinne's brother. Esmae sent him away from Kali because he is, in short, a treacherous bastard. Alas, we have not seen the last of him.

SHAY BLACKHEART, the princess and ruler of Skylark. She has something of a grudge against Kali since Lord Selwyn attempted to invade her realm (I refer you to the treacherous bastard detail above).

MIYO SAKA, Queen of Tamini and an ally of Alexi due to her family ties to General Saka.

YANN ROTHKAR, King of Elba.

VALENTINA GOMEZ, the Prime Minister of Shloka.

Immortals

AMBA, war goddess. She was one of the gods who made me. She cloaked Rama so that he could fight the duel in Esmae's place, which resulted in his death.

KIRRIN, god of tricks and one of Amba's brothers. He has chosen Alexi's side and took the blueflower from Esmae so that she could be killed. It's not that he doesn't like Esmae, but he's convinced she'll destroy her brother if she lives. Funny how that worked out.

VALIN, a god of wisdom, long dead. Amba's brother. He is not at all relevant. In fact, just forget I mentioned him at all.

TYRE, a god of justice. Amba's brother.

SUYA, sun god. Amba's brother.

THEA, goddess of hearth and home. Amba's sister.

Wychstar

RAMA KARN, the youngest prince of Wychstar. He was Esmae's best friend. He is now gone.

RADHA KARN, the youngest princess of Wychstar.

DARSHAN KARN, King of Wychstar, father to Rodi, Ria, Rama, and Radha. And me, I suppose. He took a vow of silence for ten years just so that the gods would help him build me. Esmae still doesn't know why.

RODI KARN, Crown Prince of Wychstar and devilishly charming to boot.

RIA KARN, the older of Darshan's two daughters, second in line to the throne of Wychstar.

NINA LI, or Mistress Li as Esmae used to call her. She runs the children's sanctuary on Wychstar where Esmae grew up.

Winter

RALF SNOW, the king of Winter and Alexi's ally. He gifted Alexi the territory on his planet that is now the small kingdom Arcadia. He is also the man who used his teeth to pluck the bowstring when he competed for me. I liked that.

SARA SNOW, the queen of Winter.

KATYA SNOW, the only child of King Ralf and Queen Sara.

DIMITRI SNOW, the son of a Winter courtier and now the husband of Princess Katya.

SEBASTIAN RICKARD, one of Elvar's most trusted advisors and the head of Kali's army. Of indeterminate age and known as one of the greatest warriors who has ever lived. He used to be Esmae's teacher before she lied to him and he is responsible for the curse that will ultimately be her downfall.

CASSELA REY, the former queen consort of Kali, Elvar's grand-mother and Esmae's great-grandmother. She was the one who cursed Esmae's mother. She is about as warm and grandmotherly as a blizzard.

JEMSY ROSE, HENRY ROSE, and JUNIPER ROSE, royal guards and members of the Hundred and One. Esmae is very fond of them.

SEBASTIAN RICKARD THE SECOND, Rickard's only grandson.

SU YEN WING, a general in Kali's army and a member of the war council. She can usually be trusted to be sensible.

ILARA KHAY, a general in Kali's army.

Arcadia

ALEXI REY, the golden prince, one of the finest warriors in the star system and a slightly less talented archer than his twin sister, Esmae. He believes himself to be the rightful ruler of Kali.

ABRA REY, known to everyone as Bear. He is as cuddly and fero-cious as his namesake. He fights on Alexi's side.

KYRA REY, former queen consort of Kali, mother to Alexi, Bear, and Esmae. She is the beginning of one of the many threads that led to this war.

LEILA SAKA, general of Alexi's army and his closest advisor. She was Max's teacher before she left Kali to join Alexi. Esmae often compares her to a cobra, and she's not wrong.

Dramatis Personae

(compiled by *Titania*, glorious warship and queen of the skies)

Kali

TITANIA, the heroine of this tale. A sentient spaceship. I was built by gods and I can never be destroyed or defeated. Except by King Darshan, for whom I was created, against whom I would be utterly useless. I am not at all bitter.

ESMAE REY, Princess of Kali, the only daughter of the former king Cassel and his queen Kyra. She won me in King Darshan's competition, an act that led ultimately to the murder of her best friend at her twin brother's hands.

MAX REY, Crown Prince of Kali, Commander of the Hundred and One, the adopted son of King Elvar and Queen Guinne. A young man of many secrets. He helped his father steal the crown of Kali and exiled Alexi, Bear, and Kyra. Esmae recently found out Max has been covertly protecting her brothers from his uncle's assassination attempts.

ELVAR REY, the usurper King of Kali. He is Esmae's uncle. He's a little paranoid, in much the same way that the sun is a little warm, and he has been blind since birth. He loves his family. I think.

GUINNE REY, Queen of Kali, Elvar's wife and Max's adoptive mother. She is not blind but wears a blindfold.

SYBILLA BLOOM, Captain of the palace guard, second in command of the Hundred and One. As prickly as a thorn and much more likely to cause a fatal injury. She has spent the last few years living at the palace. She is fiercely loyal to Max but has been known to keep Esmae's secrets from even him.

ASH, god of destruction and balance. He was one of the first gods and therefore is sort of Amba's uncle.

BARA, goddess of creation.

KIVA, a war god. He is not, you will be surprised to hear, related to Amba at all.

LAIKA, a raksha demon.

VAHANA, a garuda.

SORSHA, a very big spoiler.

for Henry,
who makes ours a house of neither rage nor sorrow

Sky Pony Press books may be purchased in bulk at special discounts for sales promotion, corporate gifts, fund-raising, or educational purposes. Special editions can also be created to specifications. For details, contact the Special Sales Department, Sky Pony Press, 307 West 36th Street, 11th Floor, New York, NY 10018 or info@skyhorsepublishing.com.

Sky Pony is a registered trademark of Skyhorse Publishing, Inc., a Delaware corporation.

Visit our website at www.skyponypress.com.

10 9 8 7 6 5 4 3 2 1

Library of Congress Cataloging-in-Publication Data available on file.

Cover illustrations by iStock
Cover design by Kate Gartner

Hardcover ISBN: 978-1-5107-3379-4
Ebook ISBN: 978-1-5107-3382-4

Printed in the United States of America

BOOK TWO IN THE CELESTIAL TRILOGY

A HOUSE OF RAGE AND SORROW

SANGU MANDANNA

Sky Pony Press
New York

CHAPTER ONE

My golden brother doesn't shine so brightly anymore. His armor is streaked with soot and the bow of light on his back has been doused in ash. He picks his way across the stony beach with a handful of his soldiers, checking the blazing ruins of his ships for survivors. Winter's sea roars beyond them, gray and foamy and cold.

The aftermath of battle is ugly. General Saka sent a small fleet toward Kali, presumably to test our defences or maybe just to test me, and *Titania* and I flew out to meet them. It didn't go well for them. We followed what was left of them back to Winter, where Alexi came to rescue them, but he was too late. They crashed onto this beach, somewhere in King Ralf's territory, and my perfect twin was powerless to stop it.

Almost as if he can tell he's being watched, Alexi turns away from the sea and looks at the cliffs beyond the beach. At me.

I'm on the cliff edge above him. *Titania* hovers close by. I can't see much of Alexi's expression from this far away, but I don't think it's friendly.

That's okay, Alex. Mine isn't either.

There's a ripple in the sky in the distance, a smear across the horizon. As it draws closer, the smear becomes more distinct. Ships. They're not Kali's, so they're either Alexi's or King Ralf's. I suspect the former. There's half a dozen of them, all powerful warships, and they cut across the silver sky until they stop behind my brother, noses pointed my way, black steel against the backdrop of clouds and water.

"Esmae." It's *Titania*, her voice in my earpiece. I feel her above me, engines humming, closer than before. "Come back inside."

She worries. These days, without my blueflower, I'm a whole lot easier to kill. They all worry.

The ships train their weapons on me. I can hear the sounds over the roar of the sea, the click of launchers shifting into place, the whir of machinery ready to fire. They're waiting for the order.

I don't move. *Titania* huffs in my ear, more exasperated than alarmed. "Have it your way."

I make sure the ships are in my line of vision, but I keep my attention on Alexi. He hasn't taken his eyes off me. One of his soldiers breaks away from the others and goes to him, speaks to him. It's my other brother, Bear.

The seconds tick by. The lash of the wind and sea salt, the roar of the waves, the whir of engines. Doused fires on the beach, ruined ships coiling smoke into the air. The battle smell of metal, ash, and smoke in my throat.

I wonder why I'm still here. What am I waiting for? To see what he'll do? To see if he'll give the order? Of course he'll give the order. He killed Rama because he believed Rama was me. Why in the world wouldn't he try again?

Except he hasn't. What's he waiting for?

That's when I realize he's waiting, too. He's waiting to see if I'll take that step, if *I'll* try to kill *him*.

After all, I swore I'd destroy him. A god even told me I would. I don't know what Kirrin meant when he said *destroy*, but one way or another, I will fulfill my vow and there will be justice for Rama. One way or another, somewhere down the line, I will destroy my brother. My twin. The one in the sun.

And maybe somewhere down the line is today. He's standing right there. As vulnerable as I am. I could kill him.

So why haven't I?

I reach for the Black Bow on my back, and slide an arrow out of my quiver. Alexi is out of most archers' reach, but I'm better than most archers. I nock the arrow. I slice the first two fingers of my right hand on the bowstring. It hurts, and it bleeds. Both familiar, except now neither one goes away. The wound doesn't heal. I ignore it.

I pull the arrow back. Aim for Alexi's bare throat. There's one small, lonely tremor in my hand.

Let go.

Let go, Esmae.

My hand trembles. My teeth chatter with cold, or maybe with fury. I don't let go. I lower the bow.

Bear leaves Alexi's side and approaches the cliff. He makes his way up to me. I haven't seen him since before the duel. His skin is paler than it was then, wan under its usual bronzey brown, and there's a dark bruise on his left cheek.

Bear stops in front of me. His eyes are sad, and soft. "Can I give you a hug?"

"Of course you can." I let him squeeze all the breath out of me. I hug him back and it feels so *good* that I want to cry. I feel like I haven't touched anyone like this in months. I let go reluctantly. "How are you?"

"Meh," he says, "You?"

"Meh," I reply.

He cracks a smile. He glances back at Alexi, then says, "He wants to talk to you."

I stiffen. "I have nothing to say to him."

"Please."

"No."

Bear sighs, then says, "I'm so sorry about Rama."

His name, out loud, is a cut. Is it possible to die by one thousand small cuts? I miss him so much. "Me too."

"But," he adds, with a wobble in his voice, "I can't believe this is what he would have wanted for you."

"You didn't know him, Bear."

"I didn't need to. No one who loves you would want this for you, Esmae." He points to the ruins of the ships on the beach. "Is this what *you* want for you? Really? You, who told me Wych folktales and ate honey cakes and read books under the yellow weeping trees in Arcadia? This war will break your heart. It'll ruin you."

I keep my eyes on the sea. "The folktales and the honey cakes are gone. Even if I were to look for them, I wouldn't be able to find them. There's only arrows and ash now."

"You can stop."

4

I step back, away from him. "Did *he* stop? When he pushed steel into Rama's heart, did he stop?"

"You're not him."

"No, I'm not," I agree. "I'm so much worse."

CHAPTER TWO

Rama died three months ago. Thirteen days later, I took him one last time into the stars and watched him fade away.

My world has been nothing but blood, war, and ash since then. I live it by day, dream it by night. Battle formations, sharpened swords, warriors in lines, ships in fleets, hologram maps charting out every step, strategies, arguments, allies, enemies. Three months of rage, of grief, of standing at my uncle's side as his greatest and most relentless weapon.

Everyone keeps asking me if this is what Rama would have wanted. I don't know if it's what he would have wanted. That's the whole point, isn't it? He can't tell anyone what he wants anymore. He was robbed of his chance to do that. He was the one who died and I was the one left behind, so I can only do what *I* want now. And what I want is to scream.

Every battle is a scream. Every strategy is a scream. I hear myself inside my own head. I never, ever stop screaming. Every single breath I take is a scream, building and building until it one day it will reach such ruin that my brother will shatter into a thousand pieces.

CHAPTER THREE

Titania

She's asleep. We are in space, somewhere that is nowhere. We were supposed to go straight back to Kali after we left Winter, but then Esmae fell asleep and I diverted us. She hasn't slept in three days. She needs this.

"Mother."

That's her voice. She's not awake, she just does that. She almost never talks in her sleep, but when she does, it's always that word. *Mother. Mother. Mother.* It is the phantom she never stops chasing.

I love Esmae, so I will never, ever tell her the truth.

No one knows how much I know, you see. No one guesses how much I see. Two gods helped King Darshan build me and, whether they intended it or not, they left some of themselves behind when they were finished. And, in turn, they carry some of me with them.

You know who the gods are, of course. Amba, the war goddess, and her brother Kirrin, the god of tricks. Who else could it have been but those two? They have had a hand in this war since the very start. Hubris will be the downfall of the gods, the stories say, and in Amba and Kirrin it must surely be true.

The tether between us means I can see what they have seen, be it past, present, or future. Where they go, I go, too.

I was there when Kyra Rey called for Amba and asked her to grant her third and last boon.

I was there when the king of Wychstar asked Kirrin for a way to punish the man who had wounded him most.

I was there when Amba put her hand over a bloody knife and told the woman holding it to stop.

I was there with Kirrin when Alexi Rey took his mother by the shoulders, tears streaming down his face, and said, "Mother, what have you done?"

They are always just pieces, raw data that I meticulously sift and process until I can make sense out of it.

Esmae is still asleep. Her fists are clenched on her chest and her brows are furrowed, but her heartbeat is healthy. From what I know of humans, any sleep is better than no sleep.

There is a nudge at my consciousness. It usually means someone wants to make contact with my system, so I look for the signal source. Kali. Max, specifically. He has been trying to reach me all day, but I never answer him when Esmae can hear me.

I answer now. "She's safe," I tell him. That's always the first thing he wants to know.

"I assume she's not there," he replies. He knows it's not a coincidence that Esmae is never the one who answers these calls.

"She's asleep. We'll come back when she wakes up."

He sounds tired. "How is she?"

"She's the same."

"And you?"

He always asks me that. I like that about him. "I'm very well, thank you," I tell him. "How are you?"

"The same. I'll see you soon, okay?"

"Goodbye, Max."

When I end the connection and shift my attention back to Esmae, she's awake. Only just, according to her heart rate. She blinks slowly, then looks around my control room.

"We're not home."

"An astute observation," I remark. "You were asleep, so I made the executive decision to allow that to continue."

She makes an undignified snorty sound that I have learned to interpret as a laugh. Feeling somewhat smug for getting that out of her, I set a course back to Kali.

Then, inexplicably, I ruin the moment by blurting out, "You said that word in your sleep."

Well, perhaps not inexplicably. The truth I can't tell her is clearly corrupting my data stream and making me say stupid things. Esmae doesn't reply for a few moments, but I can see how tight her fists are. She knows what word I mean. *Mother*. She told me once that it weighs more than the universe to her.

"Can you show me my mother?" she asks me.

If I had a hand, I would smack my head with it like humans do. I try to dissuade her. "Is that a good idea?"

"I just want to see her. All the footage I've ever seen of her is years and years old."

A hologram flickers to life in the middle of the control room. Its colors are slightly muted, but Esmae's sharp intake of breath tells me it's more than she expected. She steps closer. Those fists are still clenched at her sides and her eyes are wide. An assassin could walk right up to her and she wouldn't notice. I wish she could see herself. I wish she could see how catastrophically defenseless she is.

"Mother," she whispers.

Kyra Rey looks silently back at her. She has a long neck, brown skin, dark brown hair, and gray eyes with creases at the corners. Her hair is thick, long and pinned into an untidy knot. She is only a little taller than Esmae, but where Esmae is small and soft like a duckling, Kyra is more of a swan. Graceful and aloof.

I don't think either of them would like those descriptions.

"Do you think she cares?" Esmae asks me. "That Alexi tried to kill me, I mean?"

"I think it would have broken her heart if you had died," I answer carefully.

"Really?"

I believe it's the truth, but I wonder if it was the wrong thing to say. I may not be able to keep Esmae from chasing ghosts, but I certainly should not be helping her do it.

I try to distract her. The image of Kyra flickers, and I re-create her father instead. Esmae startles and takes a step back. Cassel Rey died eleven years ago, so the version of him in front of her is young, with bright blue eyes and bronze skin and an easy, kind smile.

I pluck samples of his voice out of archived footage in my database. "Esmae," I make his hologram say in his voice.

All the color has drained from Esmae's face. She reaches a hand out to touch her father and her fingers pass right through him. She snatches them back.

I don't think this is helping. I switch the hologram to Rama instead. That should be more of a comfort.

"Hey, Ez," he says in that sweet, lazy drawl of his.

"Stop it!" There are tears in Esmae's eyes. "*Titania*, stop!"

I make Rama disappear immediately. "Didn't you want to see him?" I ask her, confused. "I thought it would make you feel better. I'm sorry, I didn't think."

"It's okay," she says, still staring at the place where Rama was. "I'm okay."

Even I, a machine, know that's a lie. But I cannot comfort her. I cannot hold her hand or stroke her hair. I cannot bring the real Rama back for her. All I can do is stay with her so that, even when there is no one else, neither of us is ever alone. All I can do is stand guard between her and the secrets that will swallow her whole.

CHAPTER FOUR

Sybilla is in the dock when *Titania* and I return, and she's royally ticked off.

"We had a deal," she snaps at me. "You're not supposed to leave Kali without me! How am I supposed to be your bodyguard if your body is too far away to guard?"

"And by *bodyguard*, I assume you mean *minder*. Captain of the Keep Esmae Out of Trouble squad. Remind me what I'm supposed to get out of this deal?"

"You don't get my fist in your teeth!"

I laugh, but she doesn't even crack a smile. I look closer and see what she's trying, as usual, to hide. Fear. I relent. "I'm sorry. I shouldn't have gone without you."

Satisfied that she's made her point, Sybilla thaws. She follows me into the halls of the palace, the familiar walls and pillars gleaming white with accents of honey. "Your uncle asked to see you as soon as you got back," she says.

My uncle, the usurper King of Kali. He's the only one who is happy with me these days. Not only does Elvar believe I'm the key to his victory, thanks to a vision from the god of tricks, but I'm now the only person in the world who wants Alexi to lose even more than he does.

"Where is Elvar?" I ask Sybilla.

"War council meeting."

I stop walking. "I'll see him when the meeting's over."

"He specifically said he wanted to see you *as soon as* you got back. Which means now." Sybilla gives me a look that says she sees far too much. "You haven't been to a war council meeting in months."

"I don't see the point. What do I need the war council for? To tell me where to go and who to fight? I can figure that out myself. And with *Titania* and Elvar on my side, who exactly can keep me from doing what I want?"

Sybilla lets out a high peal of laughter. "Come on, Esmae. You can get all thorny with anyone else, but not with me. I *invented* thorny. You haven't been dodging the war council because you think you can do whatever the hell you want, you've been keeping away because you don't want to face Rickard and M—"

"Stop." It's barely a sound, but she hears me and she stops at once. She knows better than anyone just how much the dark, quiet things hidden under the thorns can hurt.

The war council has gathered in the king's study today. They're seated around the large oval table when I walk in, twelve of them including Elvar himself, and they stare at me in surprise.

Over half the group scrambles to their feet. "Princess Esmae!" someone says.

"Esmae?" Elvar's head swivels in my direction, and what's visible of his face beneath his blindfold breaks into a relieved smile. "You're back! We've been so worried! Are you hurt?"

"No, I'm fine."

He looks visibly relieved, then says, "What can I do for you?"

I glare at Sybilla, who gives me an unapologetic shrug. Wretch.

It's tempting, but I don't give her away. "I just wanted to let you know I was back, Uncle. And as I'm here," I add pointedly for Sybilla's benefit, "I might as well stay for the rest of the meeting."

"Will wonders never cease," comes an amused voice from the other side of the table. It's my great-grandmother, the old queen Cassela. "Do sit down, my dear."

The only empty seat is between Rickard and Max. *Typical.* I sit, carefully avoiding looking at either of them. Rickard puts his hand over mine, briefly, and I know what the touch is supposed to say. *Stop avoiding me. Come back to us.* Rickard has always been very good at loving people even when he's disappointed in them, but I'm not very good at dealing with how much it hurts to see that disappointment directed at me. And Max, well, that's easier not to even think about.

Lady Su Yen, one of the king's advisors and a general in the army, gestures to Sybilla and addresses me. "No one outside the war council may be present at a meeting, Princess."

"Sybilla is Princess Esmae's personal guard," Elvar replies before I can. "She goes where Esmae goes."

"But surely we're not expecting the princess to be assassinated in *this* room?"

"I agree," I tell her, "and I have mentioned many times that I don't need a guard, but—"

"Esmae, you have almost been murdered once already," Elvar interrupts me, "and I was very nearly assassinated in my own private garden not long ago, so I don't see how we can possibly be too careful. Sybilla stays."

The sun lamps above the city shine in the windows. In the distance, beyond the lamps, I can see the darkness and stars of space. I wish I was back out there. I feel exposed in the glare of the light.

"To get back to our previous discussion," says Rickard, and his voice is as deep, calm, and *normal* as ever, which makes it unbearably tempting to look at him, "the Blue Knights are definitely on the move. They intend to meet Alexi in Arcadia, if the pattern of their movements is any indication."

The Blue Knights are a group of warriors spread across the star system who follow Kirrin. They're famous for their utter devotion to their favorite god and to anyone he in turn favors. And now that Kirrin has openly revealed that he's on my brother's side, they've decided to fight for Alexi.

I expected it, so I'm not surprised. I'm more than a little bitter, though. If the last three months are anything to go by, any love Alex lost by murdering Rama is negligible in comparison to the number of gods, beasts, and kingdoms who have shifted to his side. Meanwhile, the best we can claim is an alliance with Shloka, a relatively small territory, and the fact that Wychstar, furious about what happened to their prince, won't fight for either of us.

"We have *Titania*," I feel obliged to say. I hear her agree in my earpiece, which I haven't taken out yet. "Alexi's numbers mean very little when you factor her in."

"Esmae, you know full well that the laws of righteous warfare won't allow us to use *Titania* against infantry," Rickard says, "Only against other ships and weapons. We'll be out-numbered in a battle on the ground."

"Then we need to stay in the sky."

"I agree, but it won't be easy," says Rickard. "Alexi's strategy will be to get us on the ground and neutralize *Titania* at any cost."

"Other alliances are still possible," says General Khay, a new advisor who was added to the war council after I got rid of Lord Selwyn. I like her a lot more than her predecessor. "There are at least fifteen realms who haven't yet chosen a side."

"Elba is our best option," says Grandmother. "They have enormous reserves of gold, with which we could buy the services of entire fleets of mercenaries."

"We'll invite their king to the Lotus Festival next week," Elvar says. "It will be a good opportunity to feel him out."

Shortly after that, the meeting is over. Advisors start to leave, trickling out one by one. I prepare to flee, too, before anyone can get hold of me, but then Grandmother points out the window.

"What is that?"

"It's a ship," Rickard says, squinting to see past the glare of the sun lamps.

"And not one of ours," Max adds.

Elvar's face blanches. "We're not expecting any visitors. What if it's another attempt against our defenses?"

I move closer to the window and gaze past the lamps at a silver speck outside our shields, glittering against the total void of space. The crimson and gold clouds of the Scarlet Nebula and the pale orb of Winter are on the opposite side of Kali, so it's unlikely this ship came from there. And unlike most starships, this one is shaped like a zeppelin, an ovoid with gracefully curved wings jutting out the sides. It's exactly like the ship Rama and I snuck off with once, the one that malfunctioned. The realization makes my heart sink.

It's Wych.

"What was that, Esmae?" Rickard asks me. I must have said it out loud.

"The ship," I say. "Only one kingdom has a fleet of royal ships shaped like that. It's from Wychstar."

There's a moment of dead silence, and then Rickard's watch crackles to life with a sentry's voice. "Master Rickard, there's a ship requesting entry. Do we have the king's permission to allow it past the inner shield?"

"No!" Elvar croaks. "Absolutely not! What if King Darshan has decided to move against us after all?"

"Who is on the ship?" Rickard interrupts him to ask the sentry. "What do they want?"

"She says she's Princess Radha of Wychstar," comes the reply. "And she wants to see Princess Esmae."

CHAPTER FIVE

Elvar agrees to let Princess Radha meet us on the arched stone bridge of the palace where royal visitors are usually greeted. I walk there with the others, jaw so tight it aches. At this point, I'd rather face almost anyone in the world than face Rama's favorite sister.

Rama was only a year old when his mother Queen Radha died from complications during her youngest daughter's birth. On top of that, King Darshan was still in the final few years of his vow of silence and there are almost six years between Rama and his older brother and sister, so it's not surprising that he and the baby princess Radha grew up close. I was the unexpected addition to their team of two, the newcomer to their royal schoolroom, the girl no one could quite explain the presence of.

And now Rama is dead.

When she appears alone at the end of the bridge, my heart drops. The Radha I knew was shy, with bright eyes and a sweet smile and a full face and soft curves and an endless parade of creative hairstyles, but this Radha is a ghost. Her thick hair is up in a simple, neat twist that the old Radha would have found woefully uninteresting. Her face is hollow and the soft, rich brown of her skin is almost washed out. Her dress, an emerald green shift that I've seen her wear before, hangs off her. Gold bangles gleam at her wrists and even they look like they might slide right off.

We did this to her, Rama.

"It wasn't your fault," *Titania* says in my ear.

Radha approaches us and, as protocol dictates, curtseys first to Elvar. She takes his outstretched hand. "I'm so grateful you allowed me to visit, King Elvar."

"The pleasure is ours, Princess Radha," Elvar replies, and to his credit he almost sounds like he means it.

Radha greets Guinne, who joined us before we arrived at the bridge, and the queen says, "My dear, where are your guards?"

"I flew alone. I came despite my father's wishes to the contrary, so my ship was all I could bring with me." And then, before any of us can react to that, she moves down the line with the graceful ease of someone who was born to it. "Prince Max, how nice to see you again. Queen Cassela, Master Rickard, it's an honor to meet you both at last."

Then, finally, me. Our eyes meet. Hers are just like Rama's used to be, brown and kind, and my throat closes up tight.

"Hello, Radha."

Her eyes brim with tears. "Oh, Esmae," she says. She takes my hands in hers, squeezing them tightly, and goes on in a rush, "Father wants us to have nothing to do with any of this, but I knew I had to come. I can't hide on Wychstar while my brother's murderer gets away with what he did. Let me help you."

I open my mouth to reply, but no words come out. I didn't expect this. I thought she'd grieve quietly on Wychstar and carry on with her life. That's what the girl I grew up with would have done, but then, I suppose, none of us are the same anymore.

Max glances at me and steps in. "Are you sure about this?" he asks Radha. "Are you absolutely sure you want to be involved in this war?"

He doesn't say it out loud, but I hear it all the same, the silent warning: *Your brother got involved, and it killed him.*

"I'm sure I want justice for my brother," she says. She still speaks in the same soft, shy voice I've known for years, but there's stone underneath now and I know it means there's no way she can be persuaded to go home.

There's a moment of silence, then Elvar speaks up in a decisive and much happier tone of voice. "Your offer of assistance is most appreciated, Princess Radha, and I'm delighted to welcome you to Kali. Come, I'm sure you'd like to rest. You must be tired after your journey."

His voice trails off as he and Guinne guide her across the bridge. The others follow.

I spin round to Sybilla as soon as the others are out of earshot. "I need a favor."

"No," says Sybilla at once.

"You don't even know what I want!"

"Of course I do. You want me to abandon my position as your guard and protect that interloper instead."

21

I blink at her in surprise. "Well, yes. And don't call her that."

"And to repeat my original answer: no."

"Sybilla, we have to keep her safe," I insist. "*Please*. I can't let Rama's sister die, too."

Sybilla stamps her foot in anger. Literally. "You understand that you're just like the rest of us now, don't you?" she snaps. "You're not protected by a magical flower anymore. Have you forgotten what happened in Shloka already? You can be hurt now, Esmae. You can be killed! And you want me to leave you to it? No. I refuse. Rama may be gone, but don't you dare forget that *I* am your friend too and I won't let you push me away."

When she's finished, she glares at me, brows drawn ferociously together, daring me to fight her on this.

"I'm not doing this to push you away," I tell her quietly. "I haven't forgotten you're my friend. I'm asking you to do this *because* you're my friend. I know I can trust you. I know she'll be safe with you. She won't be safe with me."

"I need you to promise me—promise me this isn't some ploy to keep me out of the way while you go out there alone."

"I promise. I swear this is about Radha, not me."

Sybilla huffs, a sound of combined irritation and defeat. "I'll give you half," she says. "Half my time with her, half with you. And when I'm not with you, someone else from the Hundred and One better be. Got it?"

I don't deserve her. "Yes, Captain."

"Just so you know," she grumbles, starting across the bridge in the direction the others went, "I will *not* be polite to the interloper just because I have to protect her."

I smile unexpectedly. "Is that what you said to Max when I first came back to Kali?"

"I am neither confirming nor denying that."

I follow her back into the royal sleeping quarters of the palace. We check in on Radha, to whom Guinne has tactfully given one of the empty suites Rama didn't stay in when he was here, and I introduce her to Sybilla. I leave them to it and return to my own rooms.

By the time I've had a bath, it's dark outside and the night lamps have the soft light of a crescent moon. I put on a sleep-shirt and check my tech for the palace schedule. Elvar has retired early for the night, Rickard has gone to visit his son's family, and Guinne and Max are at a charity banquet at the University of Erys. My own schedule has the banquet inked in, as well, but I doubt anyone actually expected me to go.

There's little chance of me bumping into anyone I want to avoid right now, so I use the rare opportunity to roam the palace freely. Well, sort of freely. Jemsy from the Hundred and One trots behind me on his bodyguard shift, trying and failing to be a discreet, invisible presence. It makes no sense to me whatsoever that this earnest, sweet boy with far less training than me is supposed to guard me, but this is one subject on which Uncle Elvar and I don't see eye to eye. "There is no such thing as too much caution," he insists.

My mind is like the thorn forest outside the palace, knotted and vicious and screaming and never, ever still. There's scarcely a thought in there that doesn't get too close to the jagged edges of the leaves, and there are no memories that haven't been swallowed up by the vicious, cruel branches of the trees. To touch any of them is to hurt. Still, I let my thoughts trace a careful path across the woods, so that I can pin down the best way to get to my brother, but I always stay away from the sharpest, thorniest places.

I end up in the conservatory, of all places. In the heart of the room, beneath moonlight slanting in from the domed glass roof, the gods' altar looks back at me.

Come closer, it taunts. *Make an offering. Talk to us.*

I take a step closer. My bare feet press into the cold of the marble beneath them, into the ridges of the gods' symbols carved into the floor. Then, an anomaly, a place where the marble is chipped and scratched. I look down. It's the wolf symbol of the god Valin, with lines gouged across it.

I step back. I don't want to talk to the gods. There is no god I have known who hasn't betrayed me.

I leave the conservatory and go to the war room instead, the parlor where the maps, charts, and tech have been set up. This is where we strategize, assess new information, and argue.

The room is empty, so I flick a hologram of the star system into the middle of the parlor and study the shapes and borders. Forty mortal countries, several planets, and an unknown number of celestial realms. I focus on the Forty Territories. Arcadia and the several territories that have agreed to alliances with Alexi are colored deep gold, while Kali and Shloka are the only two places colored red. Fifteen territories remain silver, sworn to neither side so far, including Wychstar.

I swipe across the tablet to zoom in on the Elba part of the hologram, then access all the information we have on Elba and King Yann. He's in his late forties, a relatively handsome man with dark blond hair. He has six children and is a widower. *Three* times over. And Elba's gold reserves are just as enormous as Grandmother said they were, based on the Financial Guild's data.

"I don't like his eyes," Jemsy says unexpectedly behind me.

I look over my shoulder at him, then study King Yann's face again. His blue eyes seem unremarkable. "Are you sure it's the eyes?" I ask. "Or is it the three dead wives?"

"Probably the second one," he admits.

I consider the face hovering in the air in front of us, and then I say, "Jemsy, do you want to go on a secret mission?"

"Always!"

"Good. And you'll need your brother and sister, too."

I zoom out of Elba and back to the whole star system again. I tap on the tablet and place bright blue dots on the hologram to mark where we know Kirrin's Blue Knights were four months ago, two months ago, and today. The dots are scattered all over the galaxy because Kirrin, like all the gods, has followers just about everywhere. There's even a dot on Kali to denote that there are known Blue Knights here, too, but their dot hasn't moved over the past four months. They appear to have chosen their kingdom over their god.

But the other dots show a marked difference. Their original places are scattered, but the dots from two months ago and then from a couple of days ago show that they're converging, moving closer and closer to Winter. This is the pattern Rickard meant, the movements that suggest they plan to meet Alexi in Arcadia.

I frown at the dots, tracing trajectories across their paths. The numbers don't add up. The vast majority of the Blue Knights are citizens of other territories and don't answer to Kali, so why not just travel straight to Arcadia? Why have they moved slowly over the past couple of months? The pace and pattern feel like they didn't want to draw attention to themselves, but why would they want to hide their intent to join my brother? To avoid tipping us off about their involvement? Maybe, but we've expected them to join him for months now, so it was never likely to catch us by surprise.

My eyes are raw and tired, but I don't go back to my rooms. I look at the blue dots on the hologram and then look at them some more. Somewhere in that map is a secret my brother doesn't want me to know. Sleep can wait.

CHAPTER SIX

Max shuts the door of his darkened suite behind him. He's not much more than a silhouette in this light and I can't see his expression, but the slope of his shoulders looks tired. He drops an earpiece onto the table and runs a hand through his hair, leaving some of it sticking up at the back. He crosses the suite to his bedroom and doesn't notice me in the armchair in the corner near the bed.

My mouth is dry. I was going to speak to him as soon as he came in, but now I can't make any words come out.

Max flicks on the low lamp on the other side of his bedroom, his back to me. He shrugs out of the jacket he wore to the banquet and reaches to undo his cravat.

"Max."

He turns. "Fuck's sake," he says, a whole lot calmer than I would have been if I had found an apparition in my room, "How long have you been there?"

I shrug. "We need to talk."

"You've been avoiding me for the better part of three months, but now we need to talk?" He savagely tugs his cravat off, exposing the hollow of his throat and the rapid pulse there. "Okay, have at it. What do you want to talk about?"

"The Blue Knights don't make sense. The pattern doesn't make sense."

He undoes the top button of his shirt, shaking his head. "Have you been to sleep at all?"

"What does that have to do with anything? I'm not wrong."

"Esmae," he says, quieter now, "I don't know if you're wrong. Knowing you, you're probably right. We'll study the pattern again. *Tomorrow*, when you've had some sleep."

"I'm awake now," I say, "And you're the only one who can help me figure this out. There's something here that Alexi doesn't want us to know and we need to find out what it is. Why don't the Knights want us to know they're moving towards Arcadia? They have no reason to hide that, it's not exactly a secret who they follow, so it doesn't make any sense."

Even I can hear the too high, urgent, overtired pitch of my voice. I stand up, as if this will somehow demonstrate how *not* tired I am. Max gives me a look that says he has not been convinced by this genius maneuver, but then he says, "That's a good question."

"What?"

"Why don't they want us to know they're going to Arcadia?"

I nod. "Exactly!"

And then my knees wobble and I sit down on the edge of the bed. I guess my burst of energy is over.

"You must know why I've been avoiding you," I hear myself say, not looking at him.

"No, not really."

"I know you're angry."

"I usually am, yeah," he says. "Aren't you? There's a lot to be angry about. I'm angry Rama died. I'm angry you started a war I worked so hard to prevent. I'm angry about all the other people who will die. I'm angry Alex betrayed you. I'm angry that you won't look at me anymore when just a few months ago we—"

"We what?" I can't help but bite back. "We kissed? We cared just a little too much? Where was it ever going to go? You're the crown prince and I'm the changeling no one ever wanted."

He swallows. "I did. I wanted you."

"What about now? Now that I'm the war princess, the one who undid all the work you did, the one who's forcing you to fight the boys you love to defend the father you love. Do you still want me now?" I stand again, shaky. "The day I left to take Rama into the stars, you told me you wouldn't give up on me. And I've avoided you ever since in case I look in your eyes and see that you've given up on me after all."

"How can you know what you'd have seen if you never looked? You should have looked."

"What else could I have seen? I see it in everyone else's eyes. Rickard, Grandmother, Bear. Even *Titania* wanted more from me than this, and I let her down too. My own mother has been afraid of me all my life! Soldiers died in the ruins of their ships today and you know what I saw on their faces when they looked at me? Hate. Alex is my monster, but I was theirs. All the people who have died in this war already, all the blood, all the white fire and ash, it's because I won't stop."

"Alex is responsible for the consequences of his choices," says Max, "So is Kyra. It's not your fault she was so afraid of you she sent you away, and it's not your fault he murdered a boy in cold blood. And you're not forcing me to fight anyone. I've made choices of my own. I've been plenty of people's monster."

"And the rest?"

He doesn't answer. He doesn't have to; we both know there's no defending the rest of it. He knows I could stop trying to tear my brother to pieces, but I won't. He knows the cost of my rage and ruin.

CHAPTER SEVEN

I have eighteen messages on my tablet when I wake up. Nine are the usual invitations to different events in the kingdom, one is from Mistress Li thanking me for the gifts I sent the kids at the sanctuary last week, four are from Elvar to the entire war council, one is a summary of all the previous day's news from around the star system, one is from Sybilla complaining bitterly about how implausibly nice Radha is, one is from Radha asking me if I have time to show her around Erys later today, and one is from Ilara Khay.

I stare unhappily at Radha's message for a moment before opening the one from General Khay. It's just one line.

TRAINING AT MIDDAY.

What? I activate my earpiece, which immediately connects me to *Titania*, and she says, "You're confused about the message from General Khay, aren't you?"

"How do you know that?"

"You do know I can see literally every digital thing in the kingdom, don't you?" she replies primly.

"Then maybe you have some idea about what the hell this means?"

"Hmm," she says, in a tone I know too well. It's her *I don't want to tell Esmae something* tone.

"*Titania*."

"Someone may have suggested to the war council that you should get more training in right away."

"I train all the time."

"With a seasoned general. Rickard has been in favor of it for a while, so he sent a message to General Khay last night and asked her to do it. There's a lot she can teach you."

"There's a lot a lot of people can teach me," I say, exasperated. "I *like* learning! But that doesn't explain who suggested I needed to be taught something new right now."

She doesn't answer.

"Oh my god, it was you."

More silence.

"Why? Because of yesterday?"

"Yes!" she says, too quickly. "Because of yesterday. Because you still act like you can't be killed, and you still fight like you can't be killed, and you need to learn how to fight like a person who can."

I stand in the middle of my suite, glaring at nothing in particular. "You're right," I say stonily, "But just so you know, *Titania*, Amba liked to decide what I needed behind my back, too. And look how that turned out."

Titania makes an outraged sound. "They're not at all the same thing!" When I don't reply, she huffs. "I can't promise I'll stop sticking my nose in your data, but I promise next time I'll talk to you before I send messages to anyone else. Okay?"

"I'll take it."

"Also, it's just past midday."

I groan. I take a minute to brush my teeth and get dressed in a clean set of the dark gray fitted trousers, dark gray tunic, vest like liquid silver, and silver vambraces that all Kali's warriors and soldiers wear. I zip on the sturdy black boots they made for me in the armory, almost weightless and with technology that absorbs sound, and take a shortcut down to the training fields. Which is to say I climb down the palace wall from my balcony.

General Khay and another woman are waiting for me under one of the trees in the field. On the opposite end of the field, I see Max and Sybilla with the Hundred and One, which makes me wonder who's with Radha.

"You're late, Princess," General Khay says. She's a tall black woman with brown eyes, thick black hair that frames her head in tight spirals, and a dainty dancer body that hoodwinks literally everybody into thinking she's an easy opponent. She's not. She hides an unbelievable amount of speed and skill under her armor. Today she's in just a shirt with long sleeves, gloves, the same fitted trousers as me. No vest or vambraces.

"I know, I'm sorry."

"No matter. This is Laika," she adds, and the other woman comes forward to give me a quick smile and curtsey. "I don't believe you've met before, but she's one of the finest warriors in my fleet and will be helping me train you."

"It's a pleasure, Princess," Laika says. Her voice is soft. She's soft in general, with light brown skin, a round face, a stout, stocky shape and long brown hair that makes a cloud around her face and shoulders. She doesn't have any of her armor on either.

I greet her, then address them both. "Should I take my vest and vambraces off?"

"Only if you wish," says General Khay. "We didn't wear ours because they would have been an inconvenience today. More layers to deal with."

That makes no sense to me and doesn't sound like it has anything to do with *Titania* telling me I have to stop fighting like I can't be killed. "General, what kind of training am I here for?"

"Master Rickard told me that in your training with him, in addition to war theory and strategy, you covered the practical use of all the usual weapons, wing war, basic control of a spaceship, and unusual terrain. Is that correct?"

"That sounds right, yes."

She nods. "That means you didn't have the opportunity to train in combat against unusual weapons."

I frown. "Not specifically, but part of what I learned with Rickard was how to adapt to unexpected situations. He made me practice that a thousand times."

"It's a vital skill," she nods, "but some specific training can't hurt. Here, Princess, is an example of an unusual weapon." She takes off her shirt and gloves. She has a sleeveless vest on underneath, but her arms are now completely exposed. More specifically, the mechanical prosthesis she has instead of a left arm is exposed.

She holds her arm out to me, an invitation to look closer, so I examine it with interest. I already knew she had a prosthesis, of course, but I've never seen it up close before. "This is *very* fancy tech," I say, impressed.

"State of the art," she replies. "My fine motor skills aren't quite as precise as they used to be, but this is a far deadlier weapon than my arm ever was. I lost it when I was nineteen," she adds, "in a duel against a garuda. I won, but not before he cut my arm right off. The armory fitted me with a mechanical prosthesis and they've updated it with the latest model ever since."

"I'm sorry, I know it's totally not the point," I say, "but you know that the words *I won a duel against a garuda* are amazing, don't you?"

She snorts a laugh. "Let's try to focus, Princess. You're very likely to come up against warriors who have mechanized prostheses like this one and they will rightly not hesitate to use whatever edge they have over you against you."

"Do a lot of people have tech like this?"

General Khay glances at Laika, and then says, "Not exactly like this, but similar tech, yes. Your mother, for example."

That catches me off guard. "My mother? I didn't know that. I mean, I knew she lost her right hand on the Empty Moon, so I suppose that makes sense."

"She has a mechanized right hand now." She hesitates, and then says, "Princess, you should know that I knew your mother when she was still here. Kyra and Leila Saka were the best of friends, and Leila and I trained together, so I saw a great deal of them. They are formidable enemies to have."

"My mother's not my enemy. Not really. She's on my brother's side, but she won't hurt me."

"Leila will," General Khay says. "Don't doubt that for a moment. She's a brilliant, ruthless general and she will use whatever she can against you."

"You don't have to tell me that," I say a little bitterly. "She already has."

"Ah, of course. Shloka."

"Yes."

"To go back to the matter at hand," she goes on, "It's a good idea to learn how to deal with unusual weapons. A mechanized prosthesis, for example. Or a wolf."

I scuff my boot against the artificial grass below our feet, angry that there's no end to what Alexi can throw at me. "You mean the hounds of the Empty Moon."

"Yes. With Kirrin so firmly on your brother's side, it's only a matter of time before the wolves of the Empty Moon get involved. They used to answer only to Valin and Kirrin, the rulers of the Moon, but with Valin gone, only Kirrin can command them now. Have you ever seen one? No? They're giant, celestial hounds, dangerous under any circumstances, and they will do whatever Kirrin bids them to."

"So how do we train for that? In a simulation?"

"No," says General Khay, "We will train with Laika."

"Sorry?"

Laika, who hasn't said anything since she greeted me, now gives me a quick, unexpected grin.

And promptly transforms into an enormous lion.

With an undignified yelp, I take a step back and gape at her. Her fierce golden head is almost level with mine and her teeth gleam. "You're a raksha demon?"

She transforms back, her shape blending from one to the other in seconds. Her clothes are now torn. "I am indeed," she says, wiggling her human shoulders like she's settling back into herself. "I wouldn't say I'm as strong as a wolf from the Empty Moon, but I'm close, and it's the best we can do for practice." She frowns down at herself. "I'll take my clothes off first next time. I'm very comfortable with my own nakedness, but I did think it wouldn't be fair to you to strip down without warning."

"I would have been totally fine with that, I promise you," I reply. "Whereas a warning would have been great before you transformed into a giant lion!"

They find that hilarious. Still laughing, General Khay reaches for the sack at the foot of the tree and empties out a handful of ordinary weapons. Swords, knives, a bow, arrows, an axe, a crossbow, even a mace. Nestled in the middle of this archaic pile is a shiny modern medical laser, which doesn't bode well.

"Choose your weapons, Princess," says the general.

I strap the bow and a quiver of arrows to my back, then pick up two slender swords. "I'm ready."

General Khay chooses a sword for herself, which she holds in her right hand, and Laika transforms back into her lion form. Lion demons were the most powerful of the original raksha demons from thousands of years ago, the ones who fought wars with the first gods before they made peace. There aren't many rakshas left today, but I assume lions are still the most powerful.

We move away from the tree and into more open space. I look from General Khay to Laika and wonder just how badly I'm about to be defeated. Out of the corner of my eye, I see the Hundred and One have stopped to watch, Max and Sybilla included, and I grit my teeth. Marvelous.

"This is all your fault," I say under my breath.

Titania laughs in my earpiece.

It starts well. I use the twin swords to deflect General Khay's attacks while I dodge Laika literally snapping at my heels. I'm fast, which has always worked in my favor against bigger, stronger opponents, and it keeps Laika at bay for several minutes.

Then, as if she's decided I'm ready for more, Laika pounces. She knocks me to the ground and presses me down with both front paws.

"Get yourself free quickly, Princess," General Khay orders me, "Remember, a wolf won't give you the courtesy of time to escape."

My swords flail uselessly at my sides, under the weight of lion paws. I force a leg free and kick, hard into the soft underbelly of the lion, and she jumps off me with a roar. I throw an arrow at her, which distracts her for a moment while I deal with General Khay, who jumps back into the fray now that I'm not pinned down.

Flipping her sword over in just one hand, the general brings it down. I have to use both my swords to catch hers above my head, which leaves me completely vulnerable to an attack from Laika. I look over my shoulder to see where she is, to see if I have time to throw the general off and turn to face her.

But it's not Laika who gets me. A hand clamps itself around my throat, but it has no warmth or softness or pulse. It's cold and hard. Metal.

While her sword kept my arms out of the way, General Khay used her free prosthesis to put her hand around my throat. And then, with impossible strength, she lifts me off the ground by my throat. My legs kick frantically and I drop my swords to try and pry the hand off my skin.

I can't make it shift. The mechanics are too strong. General Khay's hand tightens relentlessly and I stare at her with wide eyes, horrified by how utterly and totally helpless I am.

"Ilara," Laika says. She's back in human form. She sounds worried. "Not so tight."

General Khay loosens her grip at once and lowers me gently back to the ground. "Take a few deep breaths," she says gently. "You'll have bruises, I'm afraid. My apologies."

As I suck air back in, my heart pounding, I croak out, "How do I fight that?"

"You can't," she replies. "Once my hand is on you, you will never be able to get yourself free. If I activate the mechanics to tighten on your throat, they will tighten even if someone cuts the prosthesis right off me and they won't stop until your pulse has stopped. That's your lesson for today."

I put my hand to my throat, still sore. "That was a pretty bleak lesson to learn."

"But you *did* learn, didn't you? Next time, you'll know not to let my mechanics get anywhere near you." She pats me on the shoulder. "You did well today, and you'll do better next time. We'll do this every other day."

She and Laika pack the weapons back up and walk briskly down the field towards the palace gates. I watch them go, my hand still on my throat. The pulse in the hollow under my palm flutters wildly and my skin feels cold and thin and bruised, like paper that can be easily torn.

And then, because my luck is just that fantastic, the back of my neck prickles. I turn slowly and look back at the palace. High up, there's a figure on my balcony.

Amba.

CHAPTER EIGHT

"Why are you here?"

She's still at my balcony, the war goddess with a proud face and rich gown and armored breastplate. She turns to face me as I slam my suite door behind me.

She sighs. "I've had warmer welcomes from Kiva."

"That makes no sense to me at all."

"No, it wouldn't," she admits. "Kiva is a war god, you know. We have an ancient rivalry, he and I. I think he's just jealous that I am the one who creates the celestial weapons." She shrugs. "Does that make more sense now?"

"Amba, why are you here?" My voice is quiet, but I hear the scream inside my head, louder than ever. I can't be near her without that scream. I can't look at her and not hear the way Rama said my name as he died. "What do you want from me?"

"Are you really going to hold this grudge forever?" she asks me. "I understand how much you loved Rama, but you know full well that all I wanted was to save you."

I stomp past the balcony and tug my vambraces off. My vest follows. "You know what?" I kick off my boots with unwonted force, then turn back to her. "I'm really, really tired of you trying to justify this with *I just wanted to save you, Esmae*. You could have told me the truth instead of sneaking Rama away behind my back. You could have asked me before you threw my best friend into that duel. You could have done a lot of things. *You* could have taken my place. If you wanted to save me so badly, why didn't you do it yourself?"

"Myself?" Amba blinks, shocked. "How could I? You know what would have happened to me if I had done that. What good am I to you or anyone in this universe if I lose my godhood? What am I without my place in the celestial world?"

"Then stop acting like what you did was so extraordinary. It wasn't. Saving me cost you absolutely nothing, but Rama *died*. You let him die." I laugh sharply. "But then that's what gods do, isn't it? You stand above the rest of us and let us bear the wounds you don't dare risk yourselves."

Amba opens her mouth, then closes it again. Her face is paler than usual. After a moment, she says, "I came here to speak to you about my sister."

I didn't expect that. "Your sister? You mean Thea?"

"No, my other sister."

"I didn't know you had another sister."

"She's not a god like the rest of us," Amba explains. "Do you remember what I told you about my birth? About my father, Ness?"

"How could I ever forget your sweet, devoted father? The one who planned to swallow you as soon as you were born?" I cross my arms over my body, putting more distance between us. "I know a great beast hid you, devoured the star you were born from, and told him she'd devoured you, too. You told me that."

"Her name was Devaki," says Amba, her tone softer than I've ever heard it, "and she was the only mother I've ever known. Gods don't have mothers the way you mortals do, but I did. She was a huge, great beast with a horned head and wings and jeweled scales, but she loved me and she raised me." She sighs and turns away to look out over the palace grounds and the city beyond, clenching her hands on the balcony railing. "I killed Ness years later, to save the brothers and sister he had swallowed before me. With his dying breath, he cursed not me but Devaki. *You made sure my daughter would be the death of me,* he said, *so I curse you so that your daughter will be the death of you.*"

I watch her hands, the knuckles white on the rail, and for the first time in months I find it difficult to hate her. "What happened?"

"Some years after that, my sister Sorsha was born. A great beast like our mother. But she was born with an insatiable hunger. You know the great beasts ate stars, yes? They devoured only what they needed and no more, but Sorsha couldn't stop herself. No matter how many stars she swallowed, she still craved more. We all knew that eventually she would devour every star, every sun. That was my father's curse, to end the world simply because I removed him from it. And to make sure Devaki suffered more than anyone.

42

"Many of the other gods came to me. They said Sorsha needed to be stopped by any means necessary. They were right, of course, but I refused to kill my sister. I refused to break my mother's heart. My brothers and Thea stood by me and promised to help me find another way. All except my brother Suya, the sun god. He went after Sorsha."

I object. "How? I always thought only one of the first seven celestial weapons were capable of killing a great beast. And the Seven have been locked away in the Temple of Ashma for thousands of years, haven't they? Under Ash's watchful eye?"

"Ash gave Suya permission to borrow one of the Seven. For the good of the world. Suya took the golden sunspear and tried to kill Sorsha." Amba's clenched hands are completely white now, the bones standing out in stark relief. "Devaki put herself in the way. The sunspear killed her instead."

I can see it so vividly in my mind: the golden god and his gleaming golden spear, the great jeweled beast lifting her horned head to roar, and the cold silence when she fell.

My own fists are clenched at my sides. I deliberately force them open. "And Sorsha?" I ask.

"Devaki's death made Suya agree to step back and give me a chance to find another way," Amba replies, "but Sorsha was beside herself. Her wrath was incandescent. She would have devoured Suya and everything else in her path." She stops, takes a deep breath, and turns around. "So, I imprisoned her."

"You did what?"

"She had to be stopped, Esmae, and I could not kill her. So I trapped her on Anga, the celestial realm where Devaki raised us. I constructed shields around the planet so that she can't get past them. I even forged a helmet for her to keep her hunger at bay, but the helmet draws its power from Anga and can only work if she's there."

We stare silently at each other as her story finds its way into the cracks and spaces around us, settling like snow. Amba has always been able to captivate me with stories, but even this story can't distract me from one thing.

"Present tense," I say.

"I beg your pardon?"

"You keep using the present tense when you talk about Sorsha. The helmet *draws* its power from Anga. That's what you said."

Amba says nothing.

"She's still there, isn't she? She's alive?"

"Yes."

"But the great beasts are extinct!"

"She is the last."

Suddenly I'm ten years old again, tiny and insignificant beside the ancient fossil of a great beast. I used to dream of them, glorious winged giants with their bright jeweled scales and their horned heads, soaring across the galaxy. I used to feel so incredibly sad that I would never get to see one in real life, that these magnificent creatures were gone.

"She's alive," I repeat. *Wonder.* That's what this feeling is. It's been so long since I've felt it that I almost didn't recognize it.

"There's more, Esmae."

Mistrust and dread come crashing back. Of course there's more. "What? What else are you hiding?"

"Plenty," she says tartly, back to her old self, "but what you need to know is that Kirrin and Alexi want to release Sorsha from my realm. They want to use her against *Titania*."

"*Titania* can't be beaten."

"She can be equaled. Perhaps not by any other ship in existence or by any weapon of mortal invention, but Sorsha? Yes. And all Alexi needs is for *Titania* and Sorsha to cancel each other out. He knows the odds are in his favor if she's out of the equation."

"They want to unleash the beast the gods have been terrified of for hundreds of years?" I ask incredulously.

"Kirrin thinks he can use *his* power to keep her helmet active, and therefore that he can keep her hunger in check," says Amba. "And he may be right, but I think it extremely unlikely. I think her helmet's power will fade if she's freed from Anga."

"Why would they risk that?"

Amba is silent. She doesn't want to answer me, which is all the answer I need.

"I see." I make a sound that's not quite a laugh. "They're more afraid of me than they are of Sorsha."

"You vowed to destroy Alexi, Esmae. You are relentless fury with the most powerful starship in the galaxy at your back. How did you expect them to feel about you?"

Somewhere in the mess that my heart has become, I feel a fierce, savage satisfaction. *Good. Let them be afraid of me.*

"Can we stop them? From releasing her?"

Amba nods. "I am going back to Anga now and I will remain there until this is over. Kirrin can't get to Sorsha if I'm there."

"Fine. Good luck."

"Try to stay alive while I'm gone," she adds. "And it would be best not to call for me unless you really, truly need me."

"You needn't worry," I say, turning away, "I won't be calling for you at all."

CHAPTER NINE

I've gotten really good at avoiding people, so it's a whole three days before Radha gets me to take her on the tour of Erys she requested. We decide to take one of the chariots instead of a starship, so that it's easy to move around on foot when we need to. Sybilla comes with us, of course, and glowers at the back of Radha's head the whole time.

"Thank you for this, Esmae," Radha says to me, as I plot a route in the chariot's system. "We haven't really had a chance to talk since I got here, have we? How are you?"

"Achy," I reply, determined to keep this light. I show them a set of spectacular bruises on my arm. "General Khay is going to be the death of me, I swear."

"I'll be honest, it's pretty hilarious," Sybilla says gleefully, "After all those months of you tearing the Hundred and One down to build them back up again, it's really, really fun to see someone else do it to you."

"You wanted me to tear the Hundred and One down!"

"We needed it," she shrugs, "Just like you need this. It's still funny."

I decide to ignore that, and turn to Radha instead. "How are you?" I ask her.

"Better since I got here, actually," she says. "I felt so helpless on Wychstar, but here I'm useful." She had access to Wychstar's sources and spies before she got here, so she's been able to give Elvar and Rickard useful information about Alexi's allies that we hadn't known before. "It's less lonely here, too. Sybilla's been such good company."

I find this almost absurdly hard to believe, and based on the incredulous look on Sybilla's face, she does too. But Radha does look better. It's only been a few days, but her eyes are brighter, some of her color has come back, and she looks less hollow. I realize that as terrible as her grief must be, it was never the grief that broke her. It was the loneliness. Just being here has done wonders for her.

"I'm so sorry," I say, "I should have come to see you after it happened. I should have spent more time with you since you got here."

"You're here now. I'm here." She squeezes my hand and smiles. "Wherever he is, Rama will like that we're together."

The chariot weaves down the white cobbled roads of Erys, and Radha marvels at the peculiar charm of the kingdom. With its red roofs and artificial forests and cottages made of materials that look like wood and stone, Kali is a true fairytale world. Beautiful and whimsical, with sharp spiky thorns underneath.

We show Radha the white domed university, the markets, the Warriors' Guild, the Craftsmen's Guild, the schools that the royal family funds, the armories. There are squares full of crowds and laughter, and roads full of old shops, and it all feels like clockwork: orderly, calm, disciplined. Every now and then, the electronic voice of the base ship updates us on temperature, airflow, and the like, but none of us pay much attention. We've all lived on ship kingdoms for too long to really notice the constant background hum of engines and electronics.

"When he was here," Sybilla says to Radha at one point, arms crossed over her chest, "Rama told us you were off doing diplomatic work for your father. Where were you?"

"Do you always ask questions like it's an interrogation?" Radha wonders.

"Pretty much."

Radha smiles. "I can't answer that." Sybilla scowls, to which Radha responds contritely, "I'm sorry. I'm very much on your side in this war, but that doesn't mean I can tell you all my country's secrets. Would you tell me about all Kali's diplomatic missions?"

"Moot point," Sybilla retorts, "we don't do diplomacy."

Radha's laughter is infectious, especially combined with Sybilla's determination to not so much as crack a smile. "I've never met anyone like you before," she tells her.

Sybilla blinks. "Is that a compliment or an insult?"

A familiar shadow passes over us. I look up and see *Titania* happily zipping around above the city, much to the glee of several children in the street. She does this a lot now. She says it's because she gets bored in the dock, but I think it's also because she wants people to see her like this. No battle, no blood. I think she wants to be able to fly over a city and not see fear on the faces below her.

Toward the end of our tour, we stop the chariot in a square surrounded by artificial canals, fountains, and shops. One of the shops is owned by my favorite chocolatier in the kingdom. There are very few places like this on Kali, because its culture has always prioritized reason and discipline over creativity and frivolity, so they feel special.

"Look, there's Prince Max," Radha says unexpectedly, pointing over my shoulder. I try not to flinch. "Let's go say hello."

She bounds across the cobbled square to what looks like a shop that sells wooden toys. Neither of us follows her. I see two of the royal guards standing watch outside the shop, which means Max is inside. I have no idea why he's there, but I can just make out his profile in the dusty glass window.

"Why doesn't she just marry him if she likes him so much?" Sybilla grumbles.

This tickles me, which is a welcome distraction. "She really gets up your nose, doesn't she?"

"She's just so bloody nice to everyone and enthusiastic about everything," says Sybilla, with such bitterness that you would have thought she had just accused Radha of murdering puppies. "She won't stop *talking* to me. I told her I was her bodyguard, not her friend, but did that put her off? Of course not! I can't promise I won't kill her, Esmae, I just can't. She keeps giving me this shy, hopeful smile and I want to hit her over the head with it. And she's so full of *feelings*. It's like she has twenty of them every day."

"Twenty *whole* feelings? How dare she!"

"Worse, she has no idea how to hide any of them," Sybilla replies, bypassing my sarcasm entirely. "When she's happy, she's practically a fountain of fizzy pastel bubbles. When she's sad, she cries. Which is a lot of the time because, to be fair, her brother's dead. So she just cries right there in front of me. And then of course I have to pat her on the back to make it stop."

"I think that's called comfort."

"It's an annoyance is what it is," she says.

I decide not to remind her of the many, many times she and I have both committed the unconscionable crime of having emotions and actually sharing them with the other. This is obviously not about Radha's twenty feelings or her shy, hopeful smile, or even her fizzy pastel happiness.

"Sybilla," I start, and then stop.

"What?"

No. She'll absolutely murder someone, most likely me, if I even hint at what I suspect is actually happening here. "Never mind," I say, valiantly squashing a smile.

"Come on," she huffs. "We'd better go find her before she throws herself in front of a chariot to save a mouse or something."

I don't particularly want to risk a conversation with Max after the night in his suite, but it would look very odd for me to just stand out here by myself. I force myself to walk across the cobbles to the toyshop door. I haven't talked to him at all since that night. I told Rickard and Elvar about Amba's visit in private, have dodged all the war council meetings over the past three days, and fought with the mystery of the Blue Knights all by myself in my rooms.

The toyshop is a small, warm place littered with beautiful wooden models, toys, and crafts. I brighten. I normally send kaju sweets and new clothes to the kids at the children's home on Wychstar, but I think they'd love the toy trains, brightly colored blocks, wooden fairytale dolls, and model spaceships I can see here.

"Esmae!" Radha materializes at my side and grabs my arm. "Come look at this. Isn't it beautiful?"

It's a small wooden tree with a dozen brightly painted birds perched on the branches. I'm about to tell Radha I agree when one of the birds catches my eye. Some of the birds are made out of wood, but some are made out of feathers and wire. This one is one of the latter, a robin, and the look of it is so familiar that I know immediately where it came from.

"He made this," I say out loud.

"Hmm?" Radha asks, glancing up from where she's examining the detail on one of the other birds. "Who did? I think the toymaker is the old lady who owns the shop."

"She didn't make this," I insist.

"It's true," a voice says behind us. It's the old lady in question, a small woman with a white bun, gold spectacles, and smile. "My hands aren't as steady as they used to be, so I don't make much anymore. Many of these toys were made by another toymaker."

"Everything is so lovely," Radha tells the old lady. "You're both very talented."

They wander off to the front of the shop, chatting merrily. I look to the back, where Max and Sybilla were a moment ago. Max is still there, crouched so that he's at eye level with a small child who appears to be in raptures of delight. He winds up a small wooden carousel. The child claps his hands when it turns and plays a soft tune as little elephants bob up and down.

Once, Kirrin showed me a wish. A galaxy of stars, bright maybes, glimmers of hundreds of possible futures. In one of them, I saw an older Max enchanting a tiny child with a toy carousel and the child had his dark eyes and copper in her brown hair. It was just one of so many tiny stars Kirrin showed me, but it was there and it was possible then. Every star was possible then.

So many of those stars have gone out now, futures that can never be. Like the one with the carousel and the child with coppery hair. Like the one where my brothers and I stood together.

And like every single one with Rama in it.

CHAPTER TEN

Titania

I watch the boy whenever I can. His name is Alexi, which means *protector*. I think about that often.

I don't yet know where he is, but wherever it is, it's dark there. I am not even certain this is happening in the present, but I think it is. I can usually tell from the way the data uploads into my system. I can usually speed up or slow down these incomplete segments of time when they are already part of the gods' memories, but I have to wait for the data in real time if I access what Kirrin or Amba see in their present. This is the latter.

Alexi Rey is the other half of Esmae, the twin I could have chosen after the competition. I do not regret that I chose her, but I do wonder what would have happened if I hadn't. Would Rama have died? Would Esmae still be alive? Would I have helped this boy take his crown? I will never know. What I do know is that he is our enemy now. So I watch him, to see what this boy will do.

There is a wooded area, full of shadows and long, thorny branches. I search my database for a match, but there are at least three different planets with trees like this. He could be in a realm on any of them.

Alexi is not alone. Bear is with him, and General Leila Saka. Kirrin, too, of course, or else I would not be able to see this. The mortals are in battle gear, pale gold vests and vambraces over black clothes, and I see swords, knives, Bear's mace and Alexi's Golden Bow. Whatever they are here for, they expect to have to fight.

"Five minutes," General Saka says to the boys, her voice low. "Then we go in."

They nod. She turns and stalks further into the thicket of trees. Bear heads off in the opposite direction, but Alexi stays behind.

"You shouldn't be here," he says to me, or rather to Kirrin. His voice is hard, but I detect worry, too. "You can't get involved. You'll fall."

"I know that," Kirrin's voice replies. "I'm just here to make sure you're okay."

"I'm not okay."

"Alex. Talk to me."

For a moment, Alexi says nothing. He looks in the direction the others went, his jaw hard. Then he says, "Did you know?"

"No matter how many times you ask me that, my answer won't change," Kirrin says. "No. Of course I didn't know. You know I'm not above tricks, but I wouldn't have agreed to that one without your consent. Alex," he adds, and holds Alexi's face gently between his blue hands, "I love you more than almost anyone else in this universe. I chose you in spite of the fact that it means I have to work against my own sister and brother. Trust me when I swear to you that I did not know."

The hard lines of Alexi's face soften. Now he just looks bereft, which is how he usually looks these days. He wanted this war, but not like this. He built his life on pride and honor, and he does not know who he is anymore.

You should have made different choices then, I tell him, but he can't hear me.

A few minutes later, General Saka comes back. "Last chance to turn back, Alex," she says grimly. "Are you sure you want to do this? We can go back to Arcadia, no harm done. No one knows we're here. I didn't even tell your mother."

"You didn't?" Kirrin is the one who replies, and he sounds amused. "Was that out of kindness or because you couldn't resist the opportunity to keep a secret from Kyra for once?"

General Saka rolls her eyes. "Kyra knows I'm more than a little irked that she never bothered to tell me she had a whole extra child. She also knows I wouldn't keep a secret from her just for my own satisfaction. Even I'm not that petty."

Alexi glances toward the thicket of trees, in the direction Bear went. I notice for the first time that his hands keep clenching at his sides. He's agitated. He and Esmae share that tell. They are both aware of it, but neither seems able to prevent it.

"We need to do this," he says at last.

"Alex," General Saka says again, obviously on edge, "We don't even know if our spy is right about what she thinks she saw in there. You can't get your hopes up."

"Too late," he says with a small smile. "This could end the war, Leila. It could give back everything we've lost."

She doesn't mince her words. "It won't give you back your sister. This won't stop her coming after you. How many visions and curses do you need to hear before you realize she will be the end of you and your family?"

Bear clomps back at that moment, which gives Alexi an opportunity not to answer. "Are we going or not?" Bear asks. He sounds excited.

"Let's go," Alexi says and leads him away. General Saka glances back at Kirrin once, then follows.

Kirrin vanishes and reappears in a small space carved out of the heart of these woods. There's a plain woodcutter's cottage in the middle of the space, surrounded by twelve guards. It's a very large number of guards for such a small, nondescript house. Kirrin has not tried to simply appear inside the cottage either, which suggests to me that there has been some kind of protective shield put over it that even a god cannot pass. I try to scan the guards' faces, but there are no matches in my database. They must be mercenaries.

Moments later, as Kirrin watches from the shadows of the trees, Alexi, Bear, and General Saka emerge from the woods from three different directions. The mercenaries don't stand a chance. Even three to twelve, it is only too easy for Alexi to immobilize more than half of them, while Bear takes on the others. General Saka leans lazily on a tree and lets them get on with it.

With the guards out of the way, Kirrin and General Saka join the boys. Kirrin approaches the house first and puts a hand up to feel for the defenses. "It's a very powerful shield," he says. I feel smug. I already knew that.

"How can we take it down?"

"Question one of the guards."

The mercenaries are not helpful. Eleven refuse to speak at all. The twelfth only shrugs indifferently and says, "There's a key that unlocks the shield. You can't get in without it. We don't have it."

"Someone must go in and out to feed the prisoner," General Saka snaps. "Someone must tend to him when he falls ill. Do you really expect us to believe not one of you is able to get in?"

She gestures to Bear to haul them to their feet, one by one, and searches them. She finds weapons, three medical lasers, a few packaged meal bars, a handful of coins.

Then, as she searches the ninth mercenary, her eyes gleam and she draws her hand out of a pocket inside his jacket. "What's this?"

It's a card made out of a metal of some kind, white with shiny blue lines. The blue lines tell me it's a data card, which means it could very likely be coded to unlock a shield.

"That looks like a key to me," Alexi says.

"It does, doesn't it?" General Saka replies, glowering at the horrified mercenary. "You lied."

"I have no idea how that got in my pocket!"

"I bet," Bear scoffs. He drops the mercenary onto the ground, puts the immobilizing cuff back around his ankle, and turns to his brother. His eyes are bright with hope. "Let's try it!"

Alexi takes the card and walks carefully to the old, battered front door of the little house. There's no handle. He runs his hand over the surface of the door and then the doorframe, searching for the lock. He peels back a strip of the wood façade to reveal a shiny tech panel underneath. His hand is not quite steady as he places the card against the panel.

The panel flashes twice and the door clicks open. Kirrin keeps to the back as they make their way in. The cottage is small but clean inside, and furnished well in shades of red, cream, and brown. I do not get to look any closer. Kirrin's attention is diverted to something on the floor.

A bare foot.

"No." Bear's voice is terrible to hear, full of anguish. "No!"

He rushes to the foot, or rather to the side of the body attached to the foot. General Saka follows him, but Alexi does not move. There is utter devastation on his face.

"Is he dead?" he croaks.

"Yes," General Saka tells him. "There are no marks on him, but his lips are blue from poison. I don't think he's been dead more than an hour."

Bear has tears on his face. "An hour? All this time, and that's how late we were? An *hour*?"

"I don't think it was bad luck," says Kirrin gravely. "I think someone found out we were coming here and took matters into their own hands."

Kirrin still hasn't looked at the body's face. My curiosity is unbearable. I want to know who they came here for.

But when Kirrin finally moves closer to put a hand on Bear's hunched shoulder, and I see the face of the dead prisoner on the floor, I wish I hadn't looked.

CHAPTER ELEVEN

The day of the Lotus Festival is bright, sunny, and warm. Of course, that's not just a happy coincidence; every aspect of the weather on Kali is planned several weeks in advance and carefully controlled, and no one would ever allow the kingdom's favorite festival to be washed out by rain.

I arrived on Kali a few months after last year's celebration, so this is my first Lotus Festival. I grew up imagining it, longing to be here. In spite of its name, the Lotus Festival is not really about the flower. It's about a battle formation. The story goes that thousands of years ago, before our star system first evolved to include human life, the first gods and the first raksha demons were at war. It got so bad that the god Ash, the destroyer, stepped forward to bring the world to an end so that the goddess Bara, the creator, could then remake it.

A handful of the other gods and a handful of raksha demons united to prove to Ash and Bara that there was another way. They created the battle formation we now call the Lotus, because of the way warriors are placed in protective petals around a central point, and surrounded the ancient celestial weapon that Ash would need to use to end the world. They expected to die for this, but then, to their surprise, Ash and Bara looked at each other and smiled. "There is indeed another way," they said. "You have proven it is possible for you to unite. It is just as we hoped."

And that was how the first gods and first rakshas made peace. Thousands of years later, we celebrate that on Kali with the Lotus Festival. Other realms celebrate it in their own ways, as well, choosing which part of the story to focus on based on their values. Kali, unsurprisingly, focuses on the Lotus.

It's a full day of starship displays and tournament games in the training fields and amphitheaters of the kingdom. Then, after the sun lamps go down, there are feasts and dances in the streets all night while the palace has a dance of its own. It's to the latter that Elvar has invited King Yann of Elba, in the hope that we can persuade him to join us.

As a child, it was at the Lotus Festival that my brothers would win every tournament. Alexi, in particular, was the star. When I pictured being here for the festival, I always saw myself with them. Alex and I would compete, of course, but the only stakes would be which of us would have to buy the drinks. Bear and I would sneak away from the dance to eat cakes on the rooftops of the market. I would invite Rama for the festivities and we would laugh ourselves silly at the grumpy old advisors who would inevitably complain that there was too much *fun*. My mother and I would be together.

I never expected to be here without any of them.

"Esmae." It's *Titania* in my ear. She sounds unusually subdued. "I need to talk to you. Can you come see me after the festival?"

I'm on the uppermost balcony of a palace tower, deeply absorbed in my favorite hobby of hiding from other people. "I can come see you now," I say. "I don't plan on getting involved in the festival. Are you okay? You sound upset."

"I don't get upset," she says, a blatant lie, "and while *you* may not have plans today, *I* do."

Things have really gotten out of hand if a sentient spaceship has a busier social schedule than I do. "Who do you have plans with?"

"The starship theater," she tells me, deeply smug. "They asked me to join them in this year's show. Keep an eye on the northern sky. It's going to be spectacular."

This makes me feel absurdly proud of her. "Good for you," I say. "I'll look out for you. Are you sure you're okay?"

"Yes, this can wait until tomorrow."

She's only been silent a few minutes when I hear the ominous sound of familiar spiky boots on the other side of the balcony door. Then the door clatters dramatically open and Sybilla stalks out, followed by a somewhat apologetic Radha.

They're carrying bottles of mulberry wine, strips of pork soaked in a spicy dark syrup, and a basket of hot, buttery flatbreads.

"We're sorry to interrupt your alone time," Radha says sheepishly, "but we decided we couldn't let you spend the day all by yourself. Not on the day of a festival as special as this. Don't you remember how we celebrated it on Wychstar?"

"With the Friendship Festival," I say.

"Exactly."

"And to be fair to you, Esmae, you picked a spot with a great view," Sybilla adds. She opens a bottle of wine and drinks from it without further ado, then squints down into the city far below. "Look, the archery tournament is starting! Are you sure you don't want to go compete?"

"I've had my fill of competitions, thanks," I tell her. "I've retired. Radha can compete."

Radha chokes on her drink, then sputters laughter. "You know I've never touched a bow in my life! That was one thing Rama and I had in common, a complete and utter lack of interest in learning how to use weapons. Father forced Rama to be tutored in the basics regardless, but he didn't bother with me."

"That's the most ridiculous thing I've ever heard," Sybilla says, tactful as ever. "Because you're a girl?"

"No, it's because my mother died when I was born." Radha's face falls. "Father pretends I don't exist more often than not."

Sybilla blinks at Radha for a few moments, stunned. I know why she's so shocked. *Her* father resents her for the exact same thing.

"Well," she says at last, "you can join the Guild of Children of Terrible Parents. So far there's Esmae, me, and most of the Hundred and One. Maybe Max, too."

"I feel like Max would not appreciate that label for Elvar and Guinne," says Radha, torn between mirth and shock at Sybilla's disloyal description of her king and queen.

"It's probably overly harsh," Sybilla admits. "They're not perfect, but they do love him."

As the afternoon wears on, there's a burst of fireworks in the northern sky of the kingdom. We look over and see the starship show begin, and there's *Titania* among the other ships, swooping and circling with unabashed joy. They create a series of beautiful, complicated formations in the sky and end with a version of the Lotus. The cheers and roars of the crowds are so loud, we can feel the vibrations all the way from the base ship.

With almost a whole bottle of the mulberry wine in me, it's easy to picture Rama next to me and trick myself into hearing his voice.

"Really, Ez?" he says, exasperated. "The top of the tallest tower? Do you have any idea how many stairs that is? You know how I feel about stairs!"

"And yet you're here," I say tearfully.

He rolls his eyes. "Of course I am. I'm resentful and grumpy and require a nap immediately, but I'm here. I'm always here."

My eyes blur with tears, so I blink them away and he goes with them.

Sybilla has her mouth stuffed with bread and pork, but Radha looks at me with a little too much understanding. "I talk to him all the time," she says softly. "It helps, you know?"

I wipe the back of my hand across my nose and say, "We need more wine."

Sybilla passes over the last bottle, which we waste no time demolishing. It's sweet and spicy and gets to work chipping away the lump in my throat.

"Where were you the other night?" Sybilla asks Radha. "I checked on you and you weren't in your bed."

"That's slightly alarming."

"I'm your bodyguard," Sybilla says, a little too defensively, "it's my job."

Radha looks confused. "Well, I have no idea. I'm not even sure which night you mean. Maybe I went to the library to get a book? Esmae might remember, we've bumped into each other in there a few times." Suddenly, she jumps up with a gasp. "What time is it? We have to get ready for the dance tonight! Do we even have time to sober up?"

She dashes down the stairs. Sybilla gives me a *you see how annoying she is?* look, and follows her. I clear up what's left of the food, pack the empty bottles into the basket, and take it all down to the kitchens. Then I go back up to my suite to get myself dressed for the dance. I don't plan to actually dance, but I'm not missing the occasion either. It's my chance to meet King Yann.

When I enter my suite, my dress for the evening is on the sofa in my outer sitting room. I stop for a moment just to look at it, to touch the soft, fairytale layers of fabric, and I feel a sudden, desperate longing for the girl who came here months ago.

When I first came to Kali, I loved the uncomplicated joy of an almost constant supply of food, beautiful clothes, and frivolous luxuries I had never had before. Hot baths, soft soaps, brightly patterned leggings just because, desserts soaked in honey, dresses made just for me. It was all dizzyingly exciting after seventeen years of small meals and thirdhand clothes.

Now I can't remember the last time I got dressed in anything other than the dark grays and silvers of my war gear.

This is the most beautiful dress the palace seamstresses have ever made me. The Lotus Festival is a special occasion, so they took special care with this. It has a fitted torso with a panel of armor on the inside and a layered, floaty skirt. There's a pair of flat golden dancing slippers on the carpet beside it. The dress itself is a creamy white, the perfect color to add contrast to and warm up my pale bronze skin.

On top of the dress is a thin, delicate gold circlet crafted to look like knotted vines. It's like the ruler and consort crowns, but smaller and gold instead of silver.

When I eventually put it on, at the end after I'm dressed, the cold vines of gold press into my forehead like the edge of a sword.

CHAPTER TWELVE

The Throne Hall has been decorated with lotus flowers for the dance, and the edges of the room are packed with small tables, chairs, refreshments, courtiers, and their families. I see Rickard with his family, including his young grandson Sebastian, who was named after him; and General Khay with two older men I recognize from her file as her fathers; and Laika with her two young children, a boy and a girl, both in identical red dresses; and Jemsy, Henry, and Juniper from the Hundred and One.

I slipped into the Hall without any fanfare, so I have the unusual luxury of a few minutes of peace. Then a courtier recognizes me and sweeps me into conversation, from which I only escape when Rickard rescues me by calling my name in his deep voice.

"I was surprised not to see you in any of the tournaments today," he says, giving me a quick hug. "Sebastian was most disappointed."

"I wanted to duel with you," Sebastian tells me. He's ten or eleven years old, with bright brown eyes and very dark brown skin. His smile is a light, utterly without reserve. "I don't *think* I would have won, but it would have been fun!"

"I agree. What if we have a duel later this week? I promise I won't go easy on you."

His entire face lights up. "That would be *amazing*. What do you think, Grandfather? Could I beat Esmae?"

"I have no doubt you could," says Rickard. Rickard, who never lies. I swallow my smile, and he gives me a sheepish shrug. He adores that boy.

Across the room, I see Radha come in with Sybilla trailing sullenly after her. Radha's in a beautiful emerald green gown, while Sybilla has swapped the grays and silvers of her war gear for identical trousers in black, her usual black boots, a white dress shirt, and a fitted black jacket. She undoubtedly has at least three weapons hidden in that jacket.

I meet them in the heart of the room, where they both do the correct thing and curtsey. "You both look beautiful."

"So do you!" Radha replies.

Sybilla, however, wrinkles her nose. "You look so *princessy*."

I snort a laugh. "Thanks."

Elvar and Guinne are announced, along with King Yann. He looks just like the pictures I've seen, and he smiles as he follows them in. It's the easy, confident smile of someone who knows he is wanted more than he wants to be here. They sit down at the high table that's replaced the thrones for the night, and I adopt an expression of polite curiosity before leading Radha and Sybilla up to join them.

"King Yann," says Elvar, once we've greeted him, "Allow me to introduce you to Princess Esmae, my niece."

"Your reputation precedes you, Princess," the other king says, lifting my hand briefly to his lips.

"As does yours, King Yann," I say, showing all my teeth in a smile.

He and Radha have met before, so they chat briefly about how their respective families are. Sybilla pours herself a very big glass of mulberry wine from the jug on the table, then says something to one of the guards flanking the high table. Guinne asks me to describe my dress for her. Meanwhile, Elvar taps a nervous rhythm on the table.

Grandmother and Max arrive together. My great-grandmother is regal in scarlet, while Max is dressed in black with a white shirt under his jacket. Grandmother takes an empty seat beside Guinne, which leaves Max to sit next to me. I fidget with the edges of the white tablecloth.

"So this is the crown prince," King Yann says, and the tone of his voice makes me look up.

Max is polite. "I am."

"You look so much like your father," Yann replies. Max automatically glances at Elvar, but Yann laughs. It's not a nice laugh. "No, not King Elvar. Your other father, the one you were named after. Max. The man your mother Maeve left me for."

There's a moment of shocked silence.

Unexpectedly, Guinne intervenes. "Maeve didn't leave you for Max," she says. "You asked her to marry you, and she turned you down. Frankly, considering you've been married three times since then, I thought you had gotten over the disappointment."

"You knew about this?" my great-grandmother demands, aghast. "And you didn't tell us?"

Guinne sighs. "I hoped it wouldn't come up."

"Do you know why I accepted this invitation?" King Yann asks, sitting back in his chair and smiling slowly. "I was going to decline, but then I decided I wanted to see *him*, the son of the woman who rejected me and the man she rejected me for. I thought it might be more satisfying to eat your food, enjoy your hospitality, and see his face fall when I refused to help you."

Elvar's hand tightens on his glass. "So you won't join us. You won't even consider it."

"This is not my war," Yann shrugs. "You have nothing to offer me. What use to me is an alliance with Kali?"

"We may surprise you," Grandmother says tartly. "Perhaps you should think carefully about what you want, boy, because we may be able to give it to you. Better that than waste this opportunity for the sake of a petty grudge."

King Yann tips his glass to her, which isn't a reply but isn't an outright refusal either. I'd quite like to stab the glass into his eye, but I fear that wouldn't be productive.

The palace clock chimes above us, nine times. The crowd empties out of an enormous circle of space in the heart of the Hall. Across the room, on a small platform, the musicians reach for their instruments. It's time to open the dance. It usually starts with Elvar and Guinne dancing alone for a few minutes before everyone else gradually joins in.

Elvar stands and raises a hand for silence. "It has been another glorious Lotus Festival," he says to the Hall. His voice booms. He sounds every bit the proud, strong king he wants the world to think he is. "And I am honored to have served as your king for another year. Tonight, as always, we will celebrate the end of the gods' war with a dance, and this year, I am especially pleased to be able to say that Prince Max and Princess Esmae will open the dance."

"We what?" I say. I dart a look at Max, who looks back at me, just as startled.

"Get a move on then," Grandmother shoos us. She gives me a pointed look. They want to get Max away from Yann. If they want to have any chance at all at persuading him to help us, Max can't be there.

Max seems to realize this, too. A muscle flickers in his jaw, but he stands and holds a hand out to me. I take it and walk out into the open space. Everyone watches. As the musicians play the sweet, tentative first notes of an old Kalian lullaby, I pull the pattern of the dance out of my memory and twirl. It's just a sequence of movements, like a battle formation. It's slow and sweet, a hand here, a foot there, a twirl.

I try and fail to tell myself that's all it is. A sequence, a pattern. But I can feel the rise and fall of his chest, can see the frantic flutter of the pulse in the hollow of his throat. Our fingers are linked so tightly, and heat radiates from his other hand right up my back.

I've been so careful about not getting this close. I've been so careful not to touch him. Because I knew my whole body would come alive, I knew my heart would break, I knew how impossible it would be to turn away.

"Yes," he says, little more than a croak.

I blink. "Did I accidentally say something out loud again?"

"I never got to answer you that night, when you asked me if I still wanted you. So I'm answering now. Yes."

For the first time in months, I look at him, *really* look at him. His impossibly dark eyes meet mine and I catch my breath at the expression there.

The corners of his eyes crinkle in a smile. "Hello."

I exhale on a tearful laugh. I put my hands on his face and feel the roughness of his jaw. "You haven't shaved."

"You like it when I don't shave."

"I can't stop." I have to say this, before either of us says anything else. "I know you want me to, but I can't. Not even for you."

As if afraid I might vanish into thin air, his fingers tighten on my waist. "I know. I can live with that. Just don't go."

"Why would I?"

"Because you always do. You're a star hurtling at a thousand miles an hour and it's impossible to hold on to you."

I swallow. "Try."

He lowers his head like he's going to whisper in my ear, but instead, with my hair hiding his mouth from everyone else, his lips brush the curve of my ear, down the lobe, to the sensitive skin underneath. My whole body coils tight as a wire and I stand very still, fingernails pressed hard into his shoulders.

He lifts his head away far too quickly, and there's mischief in his dark eyes. I open my mouth and what comes out is, "Can we go upstairs?"

But then Sybilla materializes beside us. She glances between us with a very poor attempt to hide her grin, and then she jabs a thumb over her shoulder and says, "King Elvar wants you both back at the table. It's important."

71

And there it is. Reality. The warmth in my body goes cold. Max sighs, but he nods and lets me go.

The Hall is full of dancing couples now, so it takes a minute to get back to the high table. We take our seats and Grandmother says, "It would seem there is something King Yann wants from us after all."

"Really?" I look at the king. He's leaning back in his chair, arms draped across the armrests, and he looks amused. "And what's that?"

"Elba's army and space fleet will remain in my kingdom at all times," Yann says, "to defend Elba from whatever retribution Alexi Rey sees fit to send our way for helping you. I will, however, pledge ten percent of my gold reserves to your war, to do with as you wish. As I'm sure you'd prefer my gold to my armies anyway, I assume you have no problem with that?"

"None at all," Elvar replies. He shows none of the jittery anxiety we would be seeing if we were in private. He cares far too much about what other people think of him to make that mistake. "And what would you ask in return for this generosity?"

Yann lifts a shoulder in a lazy shrug, drawing the moment out, a gesture that can't possibly be for Elvar or Guinne's benefit considering they can't see him. It's for Max. The scapegoat he wants to throw all his bitterness over an ancient rejection at.

I'm not surprised when he says, "I need a wife."

"A wife?" Grandmother barks a laugh. "How exactly do you expect us to help you with that? We are not in the business of plucking women out of the kingdom and marrying them off without their consent."

"Queen Cassela, I do wish you would give me a little credit," King Yann says. "Of course I don't intend to marry anyone without their consent. I'd like to marry Princess Esmae, and it is entirely her choice whether she accepts or not."

I feel Max's entire body tense in the seat next to mine, and I clamp my hand down on his thigh under the table to keep him in place.

"Esmae?" Elvar says incredulously. "You want us to trade Esmae for gold?"

"No," Guinne says at once. Her voice is sharp, almost panicked, and she puts her hand over Elvar's. "Elvar, no."

"No," says Elvar.

It's unexpectedly touching, but it's also unnecessary.

"I decline your offer, King Yann," I say, "And, frankly, if you want to keep your freedom and your life, it would be in your best interests to stop talking and start listening."

CHAPTER THIRTEEN

Stunned silence. Every head at the table whips around in my direction.

"What did you say?" Yann snaps, his amusement gone in the blink of an eye.

I look steadily back at him. "Juniper?"

With a bounce in her step, one of the guards flanking the high table steps out of position and comes to my side.

She smiles at King Yann, who takes notice of her for the first time. "This is Juniper," I say. "She and her brothers have spent the past few days in your palace in Elba, making friends with your servants. I was a servant once, you know. And the thing I remember most about it was how invisible I was to all the important people around me. Like *your* servants are invisible in your palace. Like Juniper, Jemsy, and Henry were when I sent them there."

"And servants," adds Juniper, with a big grin, "*talk*."

"Your servants talked quite a lot about a queen who married a king," I tell Yann, "who remained married to him for a few years and had a child or two, and then died in a most unfortunate accident. So, the king married a second girl, and would you believe it? The *same thing* happened to her. And so, the bereft, heartbroken king married for the third time and, well, I think you know where this is going."

"Whatever you're implying," King Yann says, through gritted teeth, "you are gravely mistaken."

"Am I? Juniper?"

Juniper reaches into her hair and pulls out a hairpin. When she flicks it, it snaps open, and a tiny data chip falls out into my palm.

"Your servants didn't just talk, King Yann," I say. "They gave us footage from tech hidden all over your palace, and on this footage is your third wife's murder. They could not save any of your wives, but they made sure they put that tech up after the second queen died and they held onto the footage to make sure there would never, ever be a fourth one."

"Wait," Elvar says in horror. "Yann, is this true? The rumors all these years . . . Did you really kill them?"

Yann doesn't answer. As the silence drags on, Elvar's lips press into a tight, angry line.

"Here's what I propose, King Yann," I say. "You transfer ten percent of your gold reserves to our account immediately. As soon as we have it, I'll destroy this chip."

"And then what?" Max demands. "We just let him get away with what he's done?"

"The war comes first," I reply. "If Yann goes to prison, we don't get our gold. I have the chip, *I* decide what to do with it." I turn back to Yann, whose face is white with anger, and say, "Once I've destroyed the chip, you have our word that we will never use this information. You can go back to your throne and enjoy the rest of your life."

"How can I know you'll keep your word?"

"You can't," I shrug. "But it's a better chance than what you've got now, isn't it?"

He stares at me for a moment or two, then nods. "Give me a tablet and I'll make the transfer," he says.

And so it's done. Once the gold is in the kingdom's account, I snap the data chip in two and drop it into King Yann's wine goblet for good measure. Yann storms out, presumably to return to Elba and join the long line of people who want me dead.

"It would be very poor form to break our word and share what we know with the rest of the star system," my great-grandmother says to me, a note of censure in her voice.

"I don't break my promises, Grandmother. I won't tell anyone there's proof he murdered his wives."

"Then you're willing to let him get away with three murders?" she persists, cocking her head at me like she's trying to solve a puzzle. "You'd trade justice for gold?"

"I'll trade whatever I have to for this war," I tell her, and that, at least, is the truth. "And when we win, I doubt any of you will be sorry about the way we did it."

I get up and walk away.

My slippers are soundless on the floor of the corridors as I leave the Hall and music and chatter behind. Outside, down the steep hill of Erys, I can hear more music and laughter, the sounds of the festivities in the streets. I leave it all behind and go to the tall, spiky tower at the far side of the palace. It's deserted. I take the elevator up to Max's room, the one he keeps secret from his parents.

The door is unlocked, so I go in. It's dark, but I don't turn on any of the lamps. Around me are worktables, bookshelves, the shadows and silhouettes of toys, models, miniatures, and books. It smells like wood, paper, and lavender in here. I just want to stand here and breathe, but I can't.

There's work to be done.

Max comes to the tower to find me an hour later. I'm perched on an arched windowsill and he stands between my knees, hands on the windowsill on either side of me, and waits.

"What?" I ask.

He narrows his eyes, unimpressed with the innocent expression on my face. "Haven't you heard the news? Yann is dead."

"That's terrible."

"Yes, you sound devastated," Max says wryly. "His ship was attacked and boarded shortly after he left Kali. He was killed, but his crew was unharmed."

"Who did it?"

"His crew says the starship was just like the ones Alex uses. And the assassin who killed him wore a hood and a masquerade mask. Quite a theatrical touch." Max considers me. "The theory is Alex found out about our alliance with Elba and tried to put an end to it by killing Yann. Personally, I think his spies must be *very* close to have found out about our alliance so quickly."

"That's very worrying. We should be more careful."

Max shakes his head. "You could at least *try* to sound serious."

"Which part should I be serious about?"

"The assassination of a king?"

"He murdered three women. I don't feel particularly sad about his absence from the world."

"And what about what his death means for the people of Elba?"

"I looked into it. His oldest daughter has already been more or less running the kingdom for him. She does her best for the people. She'll be a good queen."

"And the part where you framed your brother for the assassination of the previously mentioned king?"

"I enjoyed that part," I reply.

A sound escapes him that sounds suspiciously like a laugh. "The data chip? Was that real?"

"Of course not. My whole performance in the Hall was a bluff. I never sent Jemsy, Henry, and Juniper to Elba. Their secret mission was getting me a ship that looks like the ones Alexi's been using lately."

"Who was the assassin?"

I curl my nails into my palms. *Don't think about it.* "I may have become a monster, but I'm a monster who does her own dirty work."

That genuinely startles him. He glances at me, still in my beautiful dress, exactly as he last saw me. No, not *exactly*. For the first time, he notices my hair is slightly damp, like I've been in the shower. Like I've had to wash blood off me. *Don't think about it, Esmae. Don't look.*

"How?" he asks.

"Henry piloted the starship. He flew it here, to this tower out of the way, where no one would notice. I came here an hour ago to wait for him. He picked me up outside this window and dropped me off again afterward."

"You *are* a monster," he says, but he doesn't say it like it's a bad thing. "A beautiful, brilliant monster."

I fidget with the top button of his shirt. He makes a sound in his throat that's part want, part laugh. I look up at him. "Why aren't you horrified?"

"I'm in no position to be horrified by anyone else," he says, and then there's a smile in his voice as he adds, "And I know you. I know that no matter what you do, you never punch down."

I don't know how to tell him what it means to be believed in, even as I fall further and deeper into the dark, so I say nothing at all.

"This looks good on you," he says, fingers tracing the circlet of gold vines on my forehead.

I tug on the lapels of his jacket, and he leans in and kisses me. I sigh against his mouth. He tastes like mulberries and home. I kiss him harder. It feels as vital and necessary as breathing. I stroke the back of his neck and lock my legs around him.

He breaks the kiss and looks down at me, his eyes dark and his face so naked that I can't breathe. No one's ever looked at me like this. I see *everything*. So I look back and I don't flinch. I don't hide. I let him see me, too. All my desire, my rage, my grief, the guilt. I let him see that the war isn't just out there; it's in me, too, and if he wants to escape it, he should run.

And he sees it all, and doesn't run. He says, "Bed?"

"Bed's too far away," I say and kiss him again.

CHAPTER FOURTEEN

Titania

There is one other thing I never told Esmae. You see, thirty-six days after the duel that killed Rama, Esmae almost died, too.

It has been many weeks since that day, but I will never forget it. Esmae had become obsessed with getting into Arcadia. The war council assumed it was because she wanted to kill Alexi, but I knew she didn't. I knew she wanted to do worse. What good would it do to kill him and see him remembered as a tragic hero? No, she wanted to ruin his armies, punish everyone who had taken his side, and shatter the myth that he had become. She wanted the world to see the monster she had glimpsed behind the mask of their golden prince.

So I knew getting into Arcadia was not about an assassination attempt. She told me she wanted to be able to place spies in Alexi's city, which had so far been impenetrable, and

I have no doubt that was true. I also think she wanted to be able to get to her mother. She never said so, but I know she never stopped longing to see her again.

Whatever her reasons, Arcadia was why she and I flew to Shloka that day. The architect who had built Arcadia for Alexi lived there, and Esmae wanted to see what she could persuade him to tell us.

Elsewhere, Max, Sybilla, and a handful of the Hundred and One were in a starship of their own. They had been watching Leila Saka for a few days, since Kali's spies had sent word that she had handpicked mercenaries for a task the rest of Alexi's army did not seem to be aware of. On that day, they saw her leave Arcadia and followed her in what looked like a nondescript supply ship from Winter.

They arrived in Shloka with no idea why General Saka and her two dozen mercenaries were there. Imagine their horror, then, when they saw the trail of blood and realized she had come to hunt Esmae.

I'm telling this out of order. Let me go back to Esmae. We landed in Shloka in the afternoon, and the capital city's brightly colored markets, theaters, and taverns had just started to stir. All my data on the architect, Maya Sura, suggested he could often be found in a tavern just off one of the textile markets. Esmae went there to find him while I hovered above the city skyline some distance away. We were not expecting any trouble, but Esmae still had the good sense to be armed. She never left Kali without the Black Bow and a handful of arrows anymore.

Locals gawked up at me as they passed, unjustly suspicious, and I tested Esmae's new earpiece by grumbling about it to her. She was not especially sympathetic.

When the architect eventually arrived, she didn't waste any time. "You built Arcadia," she said.

"I did," he replied, and then he recognized her. "Oh. You're Prince Alexi's sister."

"What will it take for you to tell me everything about that city?"

"I don't understand," he said, startled. "You want me to put a price on that information?"

"Yes."

"Why? Why should I help you?"

"Whatever my brother paid you to build Arcadia, Kali will pay you the same to tell us about it," she said, and added gently when he shook his head, "And I can give you a thousand silvers right now, to start. I know you're in debt. I know you need this."

Maya Sura didn't ask her how she knew so much. Instead, he said, "Do you really believe me so easy to buy?"

"I don't know. Are you?"

In answer, he turned to leave the tavern. Esmae didn't move. She just waited and, just a few steps away from the door, the architect stopped, turned, and came back. He sighed. "The thousand silvers first, then I talk."

Esmae handed him a white data card. He tapped it against his watch, checked that the amount on it was correct, and closed his hand tightly over it.

He sighed. "They didn't pay me to build Arcadia."

"What?"

"I built Prince Alexi's city as a favor to the trickster god." The care with which Maya Sura said the words made it clear that he didn't want to say Kirrin's name out loud. He didn't want to draw Kirrin's attention to this conversation. "Years ago, he granted me a boon and I promised him a favor in return."

Esmae said nothing, but her hand absently tugged on a lock of her hair, right where her blueflower jewel used to be. I knew she was thinking about how Kirrin seemed to like collecting favors he could call in when he needed them.

"What does that mean for me?" Maya Sura went on. "You said you would pay me whatever Alexi did."

"Don't worry," Esmae said, "You'll still get paid, if you give me information I can use. Does another ten thousand silvers sound fair?"

He swallowed. "What do you want to know?"

"Let's start with how I can get into that city without my brother's permission or knowledge."

"I can't tell you how to get past any defenses he's put up since I created the city. That kind of tech isn't my area of expertise."

"What *can* you tell me, then?"

Maya Sura did not speak for several moments. When he did, his voice was very low. "It's not real."

Esmae frowned. "What's not real?"

"Arcadia."

"What do you mean?" My sensors in her earpiece picked up the way her pulse jumped.

"It's a city of illusions. The entire city is one large, intricate illusion. That was what the trickster god and Prince Alexi asked me to build. Not a city. A trick. I built a small, beautiful palace at the heart of it, where he lives and where the generator that controls the illusion is kept. I also built a set of townhouses and barracks outside the city gates for his soldiers and allies. That's all. The rest is a lie."

"That's impossible."

"Think about it. Haven't you noticed the whole city resembles Erys, the capital of Kali? Your brother wanted it that way. But Arcadia is just over a year old. Do you think a city with a structure like Erys's can be created in just a matter of months? Do you think the lush, grassy farms and fields could have become so bountiful in a snowy climate? The thriving markets? The thousands of civilians leading full, busy lives? No," he said again, "*That* is what is impossible."

"But I've been there, several times," Esmae insisted, her voice full of an almost desperate denial.

Maya Sura looked at her with pity. "Have you? Which part of Arcadia have you visited? The woods with the yellow weeping trees?" When Esmae didn't reply, her fists tightly clenched on the table, he nodded. "So you see now."

"The woods are real, but they're outside the shield."

"Yes. The woods, the townhouses, the barracks. All right outside the shield, where you and everyone else can be tricked into seeing the illusion I constructed. If you got past the shield, you would see the reality. Snow, rock, and a palace. He does not allow anyone but his family, his most trusted generals, and a mere handful of staff beyond the shield. Everyone else is told he wants to keep his city free of the violence of war and so no one is permitted beyond its gates until the war is over. The civilians are illusions. The cottages and smoking chimneys and markets are illusions. There is nothing in Arcadia. Just a prince, his fleet of ships, and his legions of soldiers."

I objected. "Tell him I've been there, too. I've registered heat signatures, heartbeats, all the signs of a real city."

"I'm a very good architect," Maya Sura replied when Esmae repeated this to him. "I left no detail to chance."

"The honey cakes," Esmae said quietly. "They told me they got the honey cakes from a local woman."

"Honey cakes? Prince Abra probably made them himself. Your younger brother likes to cook."

I heard the catch in her breath. I had no idea why she was upset. Wasn't this good news? We had real information we could use against Alexi.

Of course, if this was true, it meant her brothers had lied to her for months. They were supposed to have been on the same side then, but they had lied. Even Bear. And Rickard must have known the truth, too. Not at the start, perhaps, but he must have surely found out at some point? Before Rama's death, he had gone to Arcadia every week to teach her brothers. He could not have visited their palace without getting past the shield and seeing beyond the illusion, but he had never said a word to her.

Yes, I suppose I can now see why Esmae was upset.

Eventually, Esmae said, "Why? Why such an elaborate deception?"

"How did the rest of the star system react to the news of Arcadia's existence?" Maya Sura asked.

Esmae understood. "Kali was afraid. And everyone else was impressed."

"Yes. To be cast out of your home and kingdom only to land so spectacularly on your feet is quite an achievement. Arcadia makes your brother look powerful. To build a thriving city so fast makes it appear like he has more money, power, and influence than he actually does. He needed people to think of him as a warrior, not a victim. He needed other leaders to think he was a worthy ally."

"It saved his pride," Esmae said. "It gave him more of the glory he's chased all his life."

"It worked. How many allies does he have now? His illusion of power has given him real power."

Tapping her fingers on the table, Esmae said, "I wonder how many of those allies would still trust him if his deception was revealed."

"If you want to expose him, you'll have to deactivate the illusion from inside his palace," the architect replied. "The generator is simple tech and it won't be guarded, but it doesn't need to be. You'll have to get past the city's shield to get anywhere near the palace. And only someone with the codes can get past the shield."

"I'll find a way. Thank you." She reached into the inner pocket of her jacket and retrieved another white data card, which she handed to Maya Sura. "Your ten thousand silvers, as promised. Settle your debts, Maya. Go live your life. Build thousands of beautiful things."

Maya bowed his head, took the card, and left the tavern.

"Do you believe him?" I asked.

"Yes," she said. "It makes too much sense, and I was stupid not to see it sooner." And then she said under her breath, bitterly, "That blind spot gets me, every time."

"Let's go home," I said, "We can talk about this some more on the way. The sooner you're out of the open, the better."

As it turned out, it was too late. When Esmae walked out of the tavern, she walked right into General Saka and her two dozen mercenaries. And at the general's feet, his eyes frozen open and his shirt soaked in blood, was the body of Maya Sura.

Esmae's voice shook with fury as she said, "You didn't have to kill him."

"He knew too much," General Saka said. She didn't sound pleased, but she didn't sound sorry either.

"I know too much, too."

"What you know is irrelevant, Princess. I never intended to let you leave this city alive. Why do you think we're here? For an architect? No, he was unlucky. A loose end I took the opportunity to tie off. We came here for *you*."

Esmae considered the mercenaries, the deserted street that had previously been so busy, and calculated how many of them she could fight and how quickly she could get to me. For my part, I left my position and tried to get closer to her, but the narrow streets and busy markets made it impossible to get lower that the rooftops. I couldn't even see them beneath the canopies and shelters.

"How did you even know to find me here?" Esmae wanted to know. "I didn't tell anyone."

"You didn't have to." General Saka looked amused. "You have a truly beautiful bow on your back. Forged by a goddess, wasn't it? Utterly beautiful. Powerful, too. And yet so easy to attach a simple tracker to."

I hissed in Esmae's ear. "Who could possibly have gotten so close to the Black Bow that they were able to plant a tracker?"

"Alex," she said softly. "I took it to Arcadia with me one time to show him."

"Yes," says Leila Saka, assuming Esmae had spoken to her. "If it makes you feel any better, he wasn't happy about it. He wanted to trust you, but I persuaded him not to let emotion get in the way of reason. After the competition, how could we be sure of you? After all, all the tracker would do is tell us where you were and where you went. If you were truly on our side, what would that matter? On the other hand, if you weren't, wouldn't it be better to know?"

Esmae didn't answer. General Saka raised a hand. All two dozen mercenaries aimed their loaded crossbows.

"More than twenty against one?" said Esmae. "The gods won't smile kindly on you for breaking the laws of righteous warfare."

"You know, I'll take that chance," said the general. "I trusted in the gods for most of my life, but then I saw with my own eyes how fickle they are. How they bestow and withhold their favor on a whim. Our worship of them is not faith, Princess, it's *fear*. And the saddest thing is that we don't even need to fear them. They cannot lay a hand on us without losing their precious immortality, so why do we still bow? The gods may have tricks, but they have no teeth."

I listened in dismay. I am capable of more atrocities than any mortal can comprehend, and righteous warfare is the reason I will never commit those atrocities. The laws are simple, but everyone knows them. *Fight when you must, not before. War must not be waged after the sun goes down. The only weapon a mortal may hold in battle is a weapon sanctioned by the gods. The weapons built into chariots and spaceships may be used against other chariots and spaceships, but must never be used against people. If a warrior is outnumbered by more than five to one, they must be allowed to withdraw from the battle if they choose. Only mortals may fight other mortals.*

It is pompous and even a little ridiculous, but it is what holds this star system together. When compassion and mercy fail, and they inevitably do, it is what prevents countries from reducing one another to dust with the press of a button.

So it was upsetting to hear General Saka speak so passionately about why she was untroubled by an act of unrighteous warfare. It made me wonder how many others think like she does. It made me wonder what would come next.

I did not think about this for long, for it was only a moment later that I heard the *clang*, the chilling sound of crossbows firing.

"Esmae!" I cried out.

Had there been fewer of them, she might have escaped unscathed. Like a dancer, she leapt in the air and twisted, arcing gracefully over and around several of the arrows. As she moved, her hands reached for the Black Bow and her own arrows. By the time she landed on the ground again, six of the mercenaries were dead and she was out of arrows. She took down three more mercenaries with her bare hands before two of the crossbows found their mark.

One arrow hit her in the chest, the other in the leg. A sound came out of her, reverberating down the earpiece, a scream that sounded like it had been inside her for a long, long time.

She fought them, as best she could, her hands sticky with blood and her teeth clenched together to silence the scream. When she couldn't fight them anymore, she ran.

No, she *limped*.

Eight mercenaries and General Saka remained, and they chased after her. I swooped overhead, trying desperately to reach her, but there were too many rooftops and too many twists and turns. Those twists and turns may have saved her life, however, because she was able to turn a corner and duck behind a market stall.

She hid there until they passed her. The woman who ran the stall was too shocked to move, possibly afraid of what might happen to her if she intervened in any way. Esmae snapped off the ends of the arrows, leaving the heads inside her, and limped out to find me.

"Go left," I urged her, "Left, left again, and then right! There's a market square there with space I can land in."

She said nothing, but I saw her go left, then left again.

She never turned right. Halfway down the narrow alley after the second left, she stumbled and fell. I said her name down the earpiece, but there was no answer.

I hovered helplessly thirty feet above her, unable to get any closer because of the tall apartments on either side of the alley. I used my tech to zoom in so that I could at least get a better look at her. Her eyes were closed. The arrow in her chest had just missed her heart, but it had torn a hole in her lungs. Her vitals were poor, her heartbeat weak, her blood loss catastrophic.

That was where Sybilla found her, just a few moments later. I assume I was the beacon in the air that led them to her. That, or the blood.

Sybilla started screaming for Max over her own earpiece. He had been tracking General Saka, entirely unaware that Esmae was even on this planet, and he came running.

I don't think I will ever forget the look on his face when he saw her.

He looked up at me, and I immediately swooped up and away, toward the square I had tried to guide Esmae to. Max scooped up Esmae and followed me. She lay like a doll in his arms, lifeless but for that faint, persistent heartbeat.

When they got to the square, Max and Sybilla got Esmae on board and I directed them to the pods in my rear wing. They ended up choosing the pod that had replaced the one we sent Rama out into space in, but I did not tell either of them that.

As soon as they closed the pod, I switched on the robotics inside and got to work on staunching the blood loss and stabilizing Esmae's vitals.

As I worked, I shut my doors and took off into the sky. Sybilla got on her earpiece to the others they'd come to Shloka with and told them to get back on their own ship and return to Kali. I noticed her hands shook. I set the kettle in the galley to boil.

It took Esmae well over a week to get out of her hospital bed after that day, but once she could, she went back to her maps and her plans like nothing had happened. She wouldn't talk about Shloka; she refused to talk about the fact that she had almost died or about the architect whose death she blamed herself for. She just went right back to her war. She was a storm sweeping across the galaxy, and there was no stopping her.

But that day, on the way home, Max stood by the pod with his bloody hand on the glass. He didn't move the whole way back. He didn't take his eyes off Esmae once.

He spoke to her, too, but she couldn't hear him. And I never told her what he said.

I wish I had told her.

CHAPTER FIFTEEN

I don't know how I expected to feel when I woke up the morning after the Lotus Festival, but *in pain* wasn't it.

It's in my neck, sharp like a needle, but then it's gone and I can't move.

I can't move.

My eyes go wide in panic, the only movement I seem to be capable of. What's happened to me?

I'm still in my dress from last night, still in the tower, still curled up on the blankets Max tossed onto the floor of his workshop. The windows are bright with light from the sun lamps. The palace is unnaturally quiet. Of course, it *is* the day after the Lotus Festival, the one morning of year when the entire kingdom sleeps in after a full night of festivities, so that does make sense.

But this, this *paralysis*, makes no sense. Why can't I move?

Someone moves in front of me and crouches down so I can see them. "Please don't panic," a male voice says calmly. "The serum will wear off in a few minutes. We just need you unable to interfere for the moment, that's all."

As my vision adjusts to the light, his face comes into focus. I've never seen him before, but the three vertical streaks of blue paint on his forehead fill me with cold dread.

He's a Blue Knight.

He has a sword in one hand and an empty syringe in the other. That pain in my neck must have been the needle, quickly injected while I was asleep. How did they get into the palace? How did they open the door and walk in without waking me?

My heart stutters. *Max.* Where is he?

I try to speak, but my vocal chords are mostly frozen. "Mmmm," is all that comes out.

"Esmae." It's his voice, *alive*. "I'm here. It's okay."

Okay? Nothing's okay!

The Blue Knight lifts me, like I'm little more than a puppet, and props me against one of the bookshelves. I can see now that there are three more of them. Max stands between two of them, his face stony, and I watch in horror as one of them cuffs his wrists together with a silver band.

"Good," the Blue Knight who spoke to me says to him, slanting his sword inches from my throat. "No one needs to get hurt if you cooperate."

"I'll do whatever you want," Max says, his eyes on me. On the sword at my throat. The top two buttons of his shirt are still undone and he's barefoot. He must have been asleep when they came in too.

I try to shake my head, but of course I can't. I can't do anything. I seethe silently, uselessly.

All that time scheming against Yann, and I missed this. The Blue Knights. They hadn't been trying to hide their path across the star system because they hadn't wanted us to know they were going to Arcadia; they had been hiding because they hadn't wanted us to know they were coming *here*. And the Knights already here, the dot on the map that never moved? I'd thought that maybe they had chosen Kali over Kirrin, but it was simpler than that. They just hadn't needed to move. They were right where they needed to be. They had waited for the Lotus Festival, fully aware that it would be their best chance to slip into the palace unnoticed.

And I missed it. As always, my brother found a way to hit me in my blind spot. Amba will be so disappointed in me.

But this is wrong. Why go to all this trouble and then inject me with a serum? Why not kill me and be done with it? I know Kirrin takes no pleasure in the idea of my death, but I also know he'll see it done because he thinks it's the best way to protect Alex. So why am I still alive?

One of the Knights puts a hand to his ear, then says, "We're clear to get out," he says. "The festival guests from Shloka have permission to get past the shields in a few minutes, so we should be able to slip out with them."

"Good," the first Knight says, turning away from me and sheathing his sword. "Let's go. Prince Max," he adds, indicating the open window, where the second knight is now standing, "Follow my companion, please."

Outside the window, I finally see it. A starship. That's how they got in without us hearing them. They never used the door at all! I try and fail to grit my teeth. *I* used that window for my own plans last night. They must have been watching me at the dance. They must have seen me come up here and realized it was a much easier way to get in than searching the entire palace for me on foot.

No, not *me*. Panic seizes me as I realize what the Blue Knight meant when he told me he had temporarily paralyzed me to stop me interfering. They didn't come here for me. They came for Max.

I try to shout, but my lips don't move and barely any sound comes out of me. Max, mindful of the first Knight's sword, complies with the order and follows the second Knight to the window. The Knight scrambles onto the sill and uses a thick, muscled arm to grip Max's manacled wrists and pull him up with him.

"*Mmmm*," I cry, futilely.

He looks back, and his eyes are anguished. "They want you to come after me," he says, "So don't. Don't play their game."

Then he's gone, out the window and into the starship hovering outside. The other Knights follow.

And I can do nothing but watch.

It must only be about a minute before I feel my jaw loosen and my hands twitch, but it feels like forever. Sensation comes back slowly, but as soon as it comes back to my legs, even only partly, I move. I stumble to the window and activate my earpiece.

"*Titania*, I need you!" I plead. "The Blue Knights took Max."

She answers immediately. "Where are you?"

"The same window from last night."

"I'll be there in thirty seconds."

She makes it in twenty-seven. I don't waste time climbing inside her control room, but instead leap barefoot onto her tail, race down her arrowhead body to her left wing, and seize hold of one of the grips there as she takes off towards the shields. The Knights said they needed to slip out with the guests from Shloka, which means they'll have to wait for the Shlokan ships. We might still get to them in time.

By the time we reach the inner shield, the Knights' ship is about to cross over.

"Esmae, I cannot fire at their ship," *Titania* says in my earpiece. "Not while Max is still on board."

"I know. I'll have to go."

"Don't be absurd," Titania replies. "How will you stay on their ship? They must have chosen it to blend in with Shloka's travel ships and it was clearly *not* built for wing war. Look, there aren't any grips anywhere on its surface!"

"I have to try. I can't just let them take him."

"But you don't have the blueflow—"

Everyone thinks I don't care that I've lost the armor Amba gave me, but that's not true. I do care. I do care that I can be hurt and killed like anyone else now. I'm always afraid.

I swallow the fear and jump.

My body slams against the side of the Knights' ship and my hands instantly search for something to grab hold of. My nails grind into a section of decorative metal over the sealed doors, shaped like lotus flowers, but the screws whine in protest and an instant later the metal flowers break off.

The ship flies away, and I fall with the flowers.

Titania shrieks in my ear, and out of the corner of my eye, I see her swoop toward me. Her right wing hits me as she dives under me, ripping into my arm, and I land on her back. The impact of hard, cold metal knocks all the breath out of me. I reach for a grip, but my wounded arm is weak, and I miss.

I tumble off her wing and fall several feet, crashing into the red roof tiles of one of the tall, spiky towers of the city. I blink up into the sky, at the stars beyond the sun lamps, and then the sky goes dark.

CHAPTER SIXTEEN

I wake up to the steady, aggravating *beep beep* of a monitor echoing my heartbeat. I'm in my own bed, in the palace, and there's a small bird made of feathers and twine on my bedside table that sends a sharp needle of pain into my heart. *He's gone.*

The wound on my arm has been lasered closed, but my entire body aches. I was six years old when Amba gave me the blueflower, so I barely remember life before it, and the past few months have been a harsh education. I'm still not used to how painful and *slow* the natural healing process is.

As I ease myself painfully out of bed, the door clatters open and Sybilla comes in. She's very pale, but as ever, her jaw is set and her eyes flash wrathfully. "Oh good, you're awake," she says, and then, unexpectedly, gives me a hug. Her fierce, almost painful grip says what she can't make herself say.

"I tried to stop them," I say raggedly.

"I know." She takes a step back and scowls. "And you shouldn't have, because I don't know what I would have done if I'd lost both of you. But we don't have time to fight about that. You've been out cold for hours and things are *not* good. The King has sent spies and soldiers into all three cities to hunt down every last Blue Knight who may still be here. I don't think he cares if they're killed."

"Even if they weren't actually involved in what happened here today?" I ask. "They can't *all* have turned against us."

"I know that, you know that, and he probably knows that, too, but he won't listen to anyone. Not Guinne, not the old queen, not even Rickard. I don't need to tell you he's been one disaster away from something like this for months."

Elvar has his flaws, but he's been a generous, reasonable, and kind king to the people of Kali for the years of his rule. I've seen the sincere warmth in his face when he asks the servants how their families are. I've watched him on the rare occasions he leaves the palace, the way the people seem pleased to see him. I've seen the treasury accounts and the increased funding for schools, healthcare, and state benefits. He loves his people.

Except there's a point where love can't quite overpower fear. Sybilla's right, of course: this was the last straw. He's been afraid for years. He had his fears stoked and fed by Lord Selwyn, who thankfully isn't here anymore, and he's been constantly looking over his shoulder since he took the throne and exiled my family. He has lost allies, has lost Lord Selwyn, was almost murdered at his own dinner table just a few months ago, and now this. His son, his *crutch*, taken from him.

"We need to get Max back first," I swallow. "We don't have a lot of time. They could kill him. And if we can get him back, Elvar should be able to settle."

"The war council is about to meet to decide what to do about Max," Sybilla says. "Shall we?"

With my body protesting every movement, I get dressed in my war gear and follow Sybilla to the parlor we've turned into a war room, where she says the others are.

I push the door open and go completely still. Because there, seated with the rest of the war council, is Lord Selwyn.

CHAPTER SEVENTEEN

"What the *hell*—"

I can't even finish. Anger and disbelief make my whole body vibrate, and it's all I can do not to leap at his throat and tear it out. Lord Selwyn. *Lord Selwyn*. The man who tried to kill me, who tried to kill my brothers, the snake in Elvar's ear, the devil I banished. And now he's back.

"We don't have time for this, Esmae," Elvar says, his voice too fast, too sharp, and overly aggressive to hide his anxiety. "I know you and Selwyn have never seen eye to eye, but you need to put that aside right now. With Max taken from us, Selwyn has very kindly come out of retirement to help us."

"He is my nephew," Lord Selwyn says to me. "I care as much as anyone in this room about his safety. If I can help get him back, I will."

His tone is scrupulously polite and there's no sign of that sneer I remember so well, but I don't believe he's miraculously returned a new man. I'm sure he does care about Max, but I also have no doubt he seized this opportunity as soon as he found out what had happened. He thinks he's safe, that he's found a way back. He thinks I won't tell them what he tried to do to me. He thinks I want Max back too much to waste time on him.

And he's right. For now.

So, I sit in an empty seat and wait. The whole war council is here, and Guinne, as well. Her face is paler than usual, her knuckles white as bone.

"The question," Rickard says, in his deep, calm voice, "is *why* they took Max."

"My nephews blame him for exiling them," Elvar says, "and they've finally found a way to punish him."

"I'm not convinced," says Rickard. "Kirrin is too old and clever to kidnap a crown prince for petty vengeance. And Alexi is no fool either. They would not have constructed a plan like this, which would have required an enormous amount of work, just to get back at Max for his betrayal of them."

Elvar throws his hands up in the air. "Then what? You think they took him because they have something even *worse* in mind?"

"I would ask Alexi myself," Rickard says mildly, "but I severed ties with him after the duel. I'm afraid we can only speculate."

I grip the arms of my chair. I try to shut out the voices in the room, the scream inside my head, the desperate desire to be able to look to my side and see Max there as usual. I need to think. Why did they take him? If I can work out why they took him, what they want, I can work out how to get him back.

There's a part of me that just wants to fly *Titania* to Arcadia and rain thunder and fire down on his false city's shields until they fall apart, and then do the same to my brother until he falls apart, too, but I can't do that. I don't want to do that, not really. My rage is colder and more bitter than that.

They want you to come after me, Max said before they took him. *So don't. Don't play their game.*

Was he right? Did they take Max just to lure me into a trap?

No. That makes no sense. I was in that tower with Max, frozen in place and helpless. Easy prey if they wanted it. The Blue Knights had every chance to kill me, or to take me with them, but they didn't. That's a separate puzzle in itself, because no matter what they want with Max, why didn't my brother use the opportunity to get rid of the threat relentlessly pursuing him? I don't know the answer to that, but the fact that I'm still alive means this can't be about using Max to get to me.

So why, then? What do they want from him?

"What about Princess Esmae?"

That voice wrenches me back to reality, and I glare at Lord Selwyn. "What *about* Princess Esmae?"

"It's no secret that my nephew cares very much for you," Lord Selwyn replies. "You do realize that the Lotus Festival was broadcast to the rest of the star system, do you not? For all we know, your brothers watched the two of you dance. Perhaps they realized that the best way to get Max to reveal all our secrets would be to threaten you."

I stare at him, too shocked to even glare. Is that possible?

"This was planned weeks before the Lotus Festival," Rickard objects. "A dance had nothing to do with it."

That much is true, but there's something here. I remember the way the Blue Knight held the sword to my throat, utterly confident that it would make Max cooperate. Another unwelcome memory tickles the back of my mind. The yellow woods of Arcadia, my brothers and I by the hot spring, the water sloshing over my toes as I told them all the little bits and pieces of information I'd learned on Kali. The war council, Elvar's plans, numbers and allies, the names of spies. Most of that information is useless now because I made sure we switched names and spies and plans after Rama died, but I also told them about Max. I told them a *lot* about Max. I told them about his strategies, his intelligence, his ruthlessness, his compassion, his influence. I told them he was the crutch his father leaned on without realizing it. I told them he was the one who held his father and Kali together.

There was no better way to fracture Elvar, and his hold on Kali, than taking Max away.

And on top of that, what if they can make him talk? He knows almost all there is to know about this war. What if they can make him tell them all about our new plans, our new spies, our latest shield codes, all of it? If they can use the threat of a sword at my throat, if they can hold him in a prison cell in their palace and remind him how easy it was for the Blue Knights to get to me last time, they may be able to persuade him to tell them *everything*.

"He'll choose Kali," I say, out loud.

Everyone looks at me. "What was that?" Elvar asks.

"If Alex hoped to get Max to tell him all Kali's secrets by threatening me, Lord Selwyn, it won't work. Your theory may be correct, but it's doomed to failure. Max will choose Kali."

"Are you sure about that?" Lord Selwyn asks.

"Yes. I am. And if you knew your nephew at all, you would be, too." I stand, wincing as the abrupt movement pulls on every one of my sore muscles. "Look, this is getting us nowhere. We don't know how long they'll keep Max alive."

"If he even *is* still alive," says Lady Su Yen and then winces guiltily when Guinne lets out a muffled noise of distress.

"He's alive," I say, because the alternative is unthinkable. "We need to get him back."

"How?" Rickard asks gently. "We don't know if they took him to Arcadia. We don't know how many armies Alexi has lined up to meet us if we go blazing in. We don't know much of anything and that, I'm afraid, will doom us to failure and Max to death if we fail."

"So we do nothing?"

"Of course not. We cannot and will not do *nothing*, but we need time and information."

Everyone is nodding, and the truth is, I should be, too. He's right. Rickard is older than anyone knows. His skills in warfare are almost without equal, his knowledge unparalleled. He knows what he's talking about, far better than I do after a mere few years as his student, and yet I can't nod. I can't agree to *waiting*, even if that makes the most sense. The girl who would have waited because it made more sense, because Rickard said so, died months ago.

The girl I am today was born out of that duel, out of murder, hate, and grief, and she can't, *won't*, lose anyone else.

I cut a look at Sybilla, and her grim expression tells me she knows exactly what I'm thinking and she's thinking it, too. We can't wait for information to trickle in. We have to find him.

"What about Amba?" Elvar says suddenly, spinning on his heel to face me. "Can you not call on her for help, Esmae? We know she favors you."

The sound of her name makes my chest ache and it takes me a moment to realize I miss her. In spite of everything, I miss her.

"She won't interfere if it'll cost her her godhood," I say.

"It's not impossible. The god Valin made that sacrifice for Kali the last time we were at war."

"That's not a good example," I tell Elvar. "He was Amba's brother. She doesn't approve of his choice. It's a moot point, anyway. You know she can't leave Anga until the war is over. If she leaves, she risks Kirrin setting Sorsha loose. I don't know about you, Uncle, but I, for one, would prefer not to lose *Titania* to that battle."

It's not just that I need *Titania* at my side in this war. I worry about her, too. She can't be destroyed, everyone knows that, but what if Sorsha can still hurt her in some way? She's a great beast, a celestial creature of enormous power. She can devour *stars*. Who's to say she can't find a way to break *Titania*? And *Titania*, the warship who never wanted a war, deserves better than that. So no, I can't risk throwing her into Sorsha's jaws. Not if there's another way.

The war council goes their separate ways after that. I stay behind just for a moment and confront Lord Selwyn. "We had a deal."

"He's my nephew. I couldn't ignore my sister's plea for help." He gives me a cold, unfriendly look. "Whatever you think of me, Princess, you need to put it aside for the moment. Max is more important."

"You seem to have conveniently forgotten that this is not about how I feel about you. It's about the fact that you tried to murder me."

"Allow me to clarify that the reason I tried to kill you was because you were working with your brother and may well have been the death of Elvar down the line. I don't have to worry about that anymore. You and I are on the same side now. Perhaps you should consider that."

I laugh. "It doesn't matter whose side *I'm* on. What matters is the only side you're on, Lord Selwyn, is your own. Maybe Guinne's, at a stretch. Rama's murder and Max's capture are not opportunities for you to exploit."

I walk away before he can reply and find Sybilla waiting for me in the hallway.

"What now?" she asks.

I take a deep, shaky breath. "Now we find another way to get him back."

CHAPTER EIGHTEEN

You would think, knowing full well that I had fallen out of the sky and crashed into a rooftop the previous day, that General Khay would go easy on me in training.

No such luck.

It starts badly. I'm with Sybilla, using *Titania*'s ability to access an almost infinite amount of data across the star system to try and pinpoint exactly where Max has been taken, when General Khay marches into my suite and demands to know why I haven't turned up to train as usual. Short of literally fighting her, which is exactly what she wants me to do anyway, I have no choice but to follow her back down to the field, where Laika is waiting for us.

So then I have to repeatedly evade an advancing lion and simultaneously fight off a talented general whose mechanized arm is only too ready to grab hold of me if I dare get too close. This is our fifth session, and I still lose more often than I win. Even years of training with Rickard couldn't teach me how to fight like someone who knows she can be killed. I took my celestial armor for granted for most of my life, and I still catch myself expecting it to protect me. It's a hard habit to break.

An hour in, every bone in my body hurts, but General Khay is not ready to stop. She wants me to advance, get past her defenses and make a move that would kill her if this were a real battle. I try, and she knocks me away. I try again, and she dodges. The practiced ease with which she moves is truly beautiful in the full midday light of the sun lamps, but I'm in too much pain to appreciate it.

"Again," she says, calm but implacable, "Again."

"Ilara, she needs a break," Laika protests, back in her human form, hands on her generous hips.

"Alexi will not give her a break," the general replies. "Did he give her a break during that duel? Did he hold back?"

His name sends electricity down my spine, reanimating my bruised, tired body. I should use that surge to fight, but instead all I can think about is the duel. I think about that final, terrible moment when I realized Rama was about to die and realized, too, that I could do absolutely *nothing* to stop it.

So I scream.

Laika takes a startled step backward, but General Khay only lowers her sword and says, "Louder."

So I scream the scream inside my head, the one I hear all the time. I scream the cold, sharp sound of betrayal and grief. I scream the rage, always, always the rage. I scream monsters out of the dark and gargoyles to life. I scream my brother's destruction, and my own, because I know, I've *always* known, that there will never be one without the other.

I scream, and scream, until my voice scrapes and falters over the sounds. And still, even after it stops, it goes on inside.

After a moment, General Khay says, "Do you feel better?"

I shake my head.

"No, I didn't think so. That kind of pain doesn't just dissipate into the sky. You scream because you have been betrayed by almost everyone you have trusted."

I close my eyes and see it all in the dark: the baby in the pod, the way the sun turned Rama's eyes gold as he died, Amba saying he wasn't important, Rickard's curse. *You stole knowledge you weren't entitled to, so when you need it most, that knowledge will fail you.* I see my inevitable end, the place where countless betrayals, curses, and my own devastating choices will come together at last.

As I open my eyes, I hear myself say, "I never stop screaming."

"I know," General Khay says gently, "and you never will, not until you can let them go. The brother who fears an equal, the mother who fears a curse, all of them. You are not ready to hear this, Esmae, but one day you will be and you will remember this then. You must learn to live your life without your mother and brother. You cannot live for love of them, and you cannot live for hatred of them either."

"We're at war," I remind her. "Even if I wanted it, I can't be free of them."

"Yes, we're at war. All the more reason to find your place in the world without them. If you want to win, you need to let them go." She taps my left temple: "Keep them in here," and then taps my heart: "Not in here. Expect no mercy from them, Esmae, and show them none in return. And never, ever turn your back on them."

When I return to the palace, I go to the Portrait Gallery, where rows of beautiful paintings line the honey-colored walls. Princesses, princes, kings, queens, consorts. An entire history of Reys since my ancestor Nalini Rey captained Kali's base ship into the sky and became the new country's first queen.

There she is, the first painting as soon as you enter the Gallery. She has thick, wavy dark hair, brown skin dusted with gold, large brown eyes, and the ruler's silver crown. Her gown is a deep, vibrant red, a color that has been worn in every painting since. A few catch my eye as I make my way down the Gallery, like my grandmother, Queen Vanya, who has a beautiful red scarf around her throat; or King Tarun, who ruled three hundred years ago, and who wears a red cravat; or Shiv, after whom Kali's second city was named, who was genderfluid and chose to wear a red silk dress shirt in their portrait.

Finally, as I come to the end of the Gallery, I find the portrait I came here to see. It's the reason I've never come here before.

I look at the intricate detail of the arched window in the background and the gilded gold edges of the frame, just to avoid having to look at *them*. Like gazing directly into the sun, my eyes refuse to do it. I have to force myself.

Bear is the easiest to look at, so I look at him first. He's only about three or four in the portrait, a chubby child with an enormous smile. Beside him is our father, King Cassel, and then Alexi, five years old, serious even then. And finally Queen Kyra, our mother. She was a nobody once, like me. She made a name for herself when she plucked a blueflower from the dreaded seas of the Empty Moon. She was an adventurer, she fell in love, she accidentally killed a queen, and somewhere in her story, she became the woman she is today. I don't know who that woman is. I'm afraid sometimes that I'll never know her, not really.

Mother. The word I sometimes say in my sleep.

They're bathed in soft, romantic light in the painting. The perfect family. Beautiful, proud, and happy. Mine, and not mine. I am not on these walls.

Let them go. Everything I ever wanted from them, everything I ever hoped for, it only ever existed in this portrait. This is the soft, romantic vision I wanted and the one I could never have had. It was always just a portrait in a gallery of ghosts. *Let them go*.

I turn to the opposite wall of the Gallery and look at the last portrait, of Elvar, Guinne, and Max. Even they seem wrong in paint and water. There's none of Elvar's fear and courage, none of Guinne's kindness and ambition. Where's the king who is terrified of shadows, yet fights for his throne anyway? Where's the queen who cast two children out of their home to keep her crown, yet opened that home to a hundred other children? And Max, the thief prince, who charts wars across the stars for his father's sake and hides in a tower to make birds out of features and wire. Where is he?

Where is he?

I turn slowly, portrait after portrait flashing by. Look at them all, the ghosts of the House of Rey. This is my inheritance, my family. *Let them go*.

Can I? Even now, even after looking these portraits in the eye and recognizing that the family in my heart is about as real and attainable as the one on these walls, I don't know. When I remember honey cakes and tentative smiles under the yellow trees of Arcadia, when I remember that word I say in my sleep, I don't feel sure of anything anymore.

They were my beginning and they'll be my end. Like Amba, who has spent centuries trying to protect the sister who could destroy the world; like the young warrior Ek Lavya, whose love for his teacher was his ruin; like the god Valin, who gave up the stars because he loved a mortal realm; and like my mother, whose love put her on a path to her own destruction. I'm just like them. I can't walk away from an end of my own making. My choices, my mistakes, my consequences.

There's no other way.

CHAPTER NINETEEN

Rama and I are playing Warlords. We're ten years old. He's not very good, but I have to pretend I'm not very good either, so we're evenly matched.

"I'm going to ask Father to adopt you," he says. "Then you can be my real sister."

Shocked, I open my mouth to tell him the truth about who I am, but I can't make myself say it. So instead I say, "You can't do that. You're a prince. I'm no one."

"You're someone to me."

I lean across the table between us, squish his face in my hands, and kiss his forehead. "That's very nice, but you still can't ask your father to adopt me."

He makes a face at me. I move a chariot on the board. When I look up, he's seventeen years old. "I was a better brother than Alexi," he says.

"I know," I say.

He moves his queen. "Warlock lock," he says. "I win."

I check the board. How did he do that?

When I look up, he's not Rama anymore.

"If you want him back, Esmae," Alex says, "you know where to find me."

And then I wake up.

CHAPTER TWENTY

Three days pass. Then a fourth, and a fifth. With each day, it gets harder and harder to be sure Max is still alive.

Nine Blue Knights are imprisoned until it can be proven, one way or another, if they were involved in Max's capture. Two others die in the attempt to arrest them and I don't think we'll ever know if they had any part in it. Kirrin will be upset when he finds out, but I don't know if he'll retaliate; maybe, when he recruited his Blue Knights to Alexi's cause and used them to take Max, he made peace with the likelihood that there would be casualties.

The Hundred and One come back from their usual trips into the city to report that the people of Erys are uneasy and restless. They're unhappy that Max is missing; they're upset that two of a god's devoted followers have died without a trial; they're worried about what's next. Kali is a warrior ship, forged by centuries of carving out survival and power in the sky, and our culture has been shaped by the warrior way. *Courage, strength, and honor.* It's what we respect above all else, but respect for the warrior way is not the same as respect for war itself.

Fight when you must, not before. That's the first law of righteous warfare. That's the first lesson. And the death of two Blue Knights who may have had nothing whatsoever to do with the country's captured prince doesn't sit well with anyone. Alexi's supporters will use it to stoke ill will toward the usurper king, while Elvar's supporters will defend him as a frightened father. Years of division are about to bear their dark, ugly fruit.

On the other hand, King Yann's death has had the effect I'd hoped it would. I killed him in cold blood for the sake of my own war as much as for the sake of the ghosts of three dead women, but I am still not sorry. I have no room left for more guilt or regret. Especially not when I see Yann's daughter take the throne with quiet dignity and announce the end of several of her father's unpopular policies. Especially not when we hear word from our spies that Alexi's allies are skittish. Some of them believed him when he sent out a broadcast to insist he had nothing to do with the assassination, but others aren't quite so certain. After all, the whole world saw footage of him killing Rama in what should have been a simple duel. If he could do that, he could do this, too. *And if he could do this,* his allies will think, *he could do it to me if I make him angry.*

He was the darling of the star system, their golden boy. By the time I'm done, he'll be a ruin.

"We still don't know where Max is," Radha says to me. We're alone in the war room, studying the holographic map of the star system. "Arcadia seems an obvious guess, but they may not have chosen an obvious place. And even if they did, we still don't know how to get into Arcadia. Do we?"

"No, but that's my next battle," I say, staring at the dot that represents Arcadia. "The shield is a problem. The architect Maya Sura said he couldn't help us get past it, and *Titania* hasn't been able to hack it, but there must be a way."

"Esmae, I know you don't want to talk about this, but what happens if Max is dead?"

My instinct is to snap that he's not, but I control myself. It's not her fault. She's worried too. Since she came to Kali, her color has come back, her face is fuller, she's eating, and she looks happier. (I think Sybilla has a lot to do with that, but I've resisted the urge to say so to either of them.) But she's different today. Today she seems paler, and she keeps twisting her hands in front of her.

"Radha, what's the matter? Is this about Max?"

She nods, but she won't look me in the eye. The Radha I have known most of her life has always been a terrible liar and this Radha is no different.

Before I can press the issue, Sybilla comes in. "Rickard is ill," she says.

I stare at her in shock. "What?" This wouldn't be such a surprise if it were anyone else, but Rickard *never* falls ill. We all assume it has to do with the boon the gods gifted him, the one that keeps him alive and healthy well past a normal mortal lifespan. If Rickard is ill, it's because someone caused it.

"He's okay, mostly. He's been confined to his bed. Elvar's orders. It's a fever, but it won't come down. The doctors are worried."

"Poison?" I say, teeth clenched.

"No. They checked."

"Then he must have been injected with a virus. There's no way this happened by accident."

Sybilla's eyes go wide. "You don't think Lord Selwyn did this, do you?"

My mind did go straight to Lord Selwyn, who has always resented the influence Rickard has had over Elvar and who is just the kind of man who would use the chaos around Max's capture to pull a trick of his own, but something's not quite right. I can't figure it out at first, but the more I look at Sybilla and Radha, the more it bothers me and then—

Radha doesn't look surprised.

Anxious, yes. But not surprised. My heart sinks. "I need to go see Rickard," I say. "You two stay together, okay? Don't let each other out of your sight and don't let anyone else get close. Rickard may not be the only target."

I leave the room and, just as I'd hoped, Sybilla follows in a huff and catches me halfway down the hallway. "What about you?" she demands. "I'll stay with Radha, but I wish you'd stay, too."

"Sybilla," I say very softly, making sure Radha is still inside the war room, "don't take your eyes off Radha. Don't let her touch you. Don't let her touch anyone else. Do you understand what I'm saying?"

There's a beat. Then Sybilla blinks at me. "No," she says. "Esmae, *no*. That's not possible."

"Not a word," I say. "Not until we know for sure."

I run the rest of the way to Rickard's suite. He's propped up in his bed, tired but smiling gently at the doctor speaking to him. His normally rich, dark skin has a pale, sweaty sheen. I stop in the doorway, uncertain. I've never seen him like this.

His rooms are full of people—Elvar, Guinne, my great-grand-mother, and at least a dozen servants and doctors—but Rickard takes one look at my face and says, "Could I have a moment alone with Esmae, please?"

Everyone looks surprised, but no one protests. I'm sure no one feels they can refuse Rickard anything right now.

As soon as the door clicks shut behind them, I kneel beside the bed and take his hand. It's so hot. "How bad is it?"

"I think this is as bad as it gets," he replies. "I'm weak, but not dead." He raises his free hand, which looks like an effort, and smiles ruefully at the tremors. "You see?"

"Will you get better?"

"No," says Rickard, gentle but honest. "I don't think I'll get worse, but I don't think I'm supposed to get better either. After all, the best way to punish a warrior is to make sure he can't be one anymore."

"You always told me a warrior is made by what's inside their heart, not their hands."

"Yes, I did. And it's true, but I must confess it's difficult to believe it right now."

I understand that. He's Sebastian Rickard, the greatest warrior who ever lived. Teacher of thousands, beloved by gods and mortals alike. He's so much more than that, but it's easy to forget the rest. Especially for him. So he's grieving what's been taken from him. For my part, I can't grieve because I can't believe it. It happened too fast. There was no blaze of glory, no battle. It was quick and quiet, so it's impossible to take in.

"Don't look so sad," Rickard says fondly, "I'm still here. I don't plan on going anywhere. You're stuck with me for a long, long time."

I put my other hand over his. "Good." Then, because we can't dance around it forever: "Do you know who did it?"

"Yes," he says, calmly, "And I think you do, too."

My chest tightens as my last hope is dashed. "How?"

"I think it was last night. After dinner, Princess Radha asked me to help her with the blanket she's sewing for the baby her sister is expecting. At some point, as we chatted, I remember her hand slipped and the needle pricked my wrist. I barely noticed at the time, but, well, here we are."

"You think the needle was poisoned."

"Yes."

"And you didn't tell anyone?"

"No," Rickard says, and sorrow settles over his face, "And you will not either. This is the outcome of my own choices, Esmae. I won't have that child punished for something I know she never wanted to do."

"You think King Darshan sent her here to do it." I think of Rama telling me their father had sent Radha on diplomatic work, of Radha's secrecy when Sybilla asked her about it. Had he sent her away to have her trained for this? "That's why she really came."

"Of course he sent her. Why do you think he wanted Alexi to win *Titania*? Why do you think he built her in the first place? He wanted a weapon so perfect that a boy like Alexi wouldn't be able to refuse it. *That*, the gods told him, was how he would see me fall. He wanted me defeated in battle, my glory stripped away, and he wanted Alexi to be the one to do it. He wanted my defeat to come at the hands of my most glorious pupil. Poetic justice."

"But *why*? How is this the outcome of *your* choices? Is this because you wouldn't teach him years ago? Elvar told me you asked for half of Wychstar as payment for your lessons, to test him, and he balked."

Rickard shakes his head. "That's not what happened. That's what he said when we realized other people had approached and could hear us. I didn't contradict him. It was convenient to both of us to let people believe his version, but the truth is Darshan came up to me that day to confront me about a terrible hurt."

I stare at him, struggling to absorb this. King Darshan wanted to punish Rickard, so the gods told him how. And I think I can guess which god. Kirrin. It always comes back to Kirrin, the architect of all of this. Kirrin, who grew fond of the small child Alexi had been and saw a glimpse of that child's future. A lost crown, a threat to his life, a war. Kirrin, who heard the prayers of an angry, wounded man and saw an opportunity. If all had gone as he'd intended, Alex would have won *Titania* and taken back his throne. King Darshan would have watched Alex defeat Rickard in battle. Kirrin would have kept the boy he loved safe and seen him to victory, too.

But then *I* won the competition. I was the wild card, the thing that no one saw coming. So Kirrin had to find another way to help my brother. Darshan had to find another way to destroy Rickard. And he did.

"Radha could have said no," I say, as tears run down my cheeks. "Look at you! She could have refused to help him do this to you."

"She could have," Rickard says, "but I think you of all people know, Esmae, how difficult it is to say no to the person whose love you have longed for all your life."

I brush my tears away. "What did you do to him?" I ask. "Why would he do all this just to hurt you?"

Rickard turns his face, his eyes far away. "I had a student once. Her name was Ek Lavya."

"*Her* name?"

"Yes. You know the stories, of course, but the stories got a great deal wrong. She was a girl."

My heart goes cold with dread. "If Ek Lavya was your student, then *you* were the one—"

I can't say it.

He nods. "Yes. I am the teacher in the stories. I had made a promise, you see. A reckless promise, when I was young and foolish. I promised your great-grandmother Cassela that I would make *her* the best of her class. Lavya was unexpected. Her raw talent was incredible, and she worked hard. No student of mine has worked as hard as she did. That is, except for you, Esmae. You have often reminded me of her."

"Don't say it," I say. "Please don't tell me you were so determined to keep your promise to Grandmother that you deliberately hurt Lavya."

"I regret that I made that promise, but it was one I had to keep nevertheless. I have to be true to my word at all times. You know that better than anyone, Esmae. I had to diminish Lavya."

I can't quite keep the bitterness out of my voice. "Did Grandmother know?"

"I think she guessed, when Lavya disappeared, but we have never spoken of it."

"What happened?"

"In those days, it was common for students to bring their teachers gifts. Lavya came from a poor family, so she had never been able to give me anything. I had never minded, but it had always weighed on her." Rickard closes his eyes as if he can't bear the pain of it, but he continues. "So when I told her she could give me a different kind of gift, she didn't hesitate to promise me anything. I asked for the thumb on her right hand. She smiled as she cut it off, but the stories make it sound like it was a sweet, sad smile. It was not. It was a smile with *teeth*. She walked away. Ten years later, we heard she had died. Amba told me she had gone to the Night Temple to pray to Ash. After years of prayer and fasting, as she lay dying, Ash appeared and promised she would have her revenge in her next life. Her last words were *Make me a man, because girls are too easily broken. Make me a king, because kings do not bow to anyone. And make sure I remember.*"

I swallow. *Girls are too easily broken*. Are we? Or is it just that more people want to break us?

"And Lavya was reborn as Darshan."

"Yes," says Rickard. His eyes are open now. "So you see, Esmae? This has been coming to me for a long time."

I go back to the war room. It's quiet inside, as if neither Sybilla nor Radha have said a word since I left. As soon as I walk in, tears flood Radha's eyes and slip down her face. "If I could take it back, I would," she says to me.

I want to be angry, but how can I? I assassinated a man in cold blood and I'm not sorry. She stabbed a man with a poisoned knitting needle and she already wishes she hadn't. What right have *I* to be angry?

So all I say is, "The next time you lie to me, you go home. Are we clear?"

"I *hated* lying to you," she says. She lets out a sob. "I'm so sorry. I wanted my father to see me, but he never did. He just saw a means to an end."

"Your father is the reincarnation of Ek Lavya, so her hurt became his hurt. He's in pain. It's not an excuse, but it is what it is."

Sybilla raises a hand to stop me. "Now hold on just one second," she says. "King Darshan is Ek Lavya? *The* Ek Lavya?"

"And Rickard was the teacher from the stories," I say.

"I need to sit down," Sybilla says. "This is too much for one day. Do you know I have gray hairs? Gray hairs! I'm *eighteen*. And it's because of nonsense like this."

"Esmae." Radha wipes her tears away. "I meant what I said when I told you I wanted to help you defeat Alexi. And I still want to help you in any way I can. So what happens next?"

I keep thinking about my dream, the one with Rama and Warlords. It really happened, that game. He really did say he'd ask his father to adopt me. What came later in the dream never happened, of course, but that's what I keep coming back to. I keep thinking about the moment Alex appeared where Rama had been and said *if you want him back, you know where to find me*.

It's too late for Rama, and it's too late for Rickard, but maybe it's not too late for Max.

"I need to go talk to my brother," I say.

CHAPTER TWENTY-ONE

I speak to Katya, the princess of Winter, and the enthusiasm with which she greets my request for a meeting tells me Alexi's been waiting for this. We agree to meet in her father King Ralf's palace, where my safety and Alex's safety have been sworn by the king's own oath.

Will an oath keep me in check when I come face to face with my brother for the first time since the duel? I'd like to think so, but I don't know. I'm afraid to see him.

I fly *Titania* to Winter and then go to the palace alone. He'll be alone, too. Those are the terms. Frankly, it's about the safest place either of us could be right now. No king in the star system would break his oath to a guest.

Princess Katya meets me in the entrance hall and guides me to a private parlor in a quiet part of the palace. She's more subdued than I remember her.

"How can you still be his friend?" I can't help asking her. "You must have known Rama. How can you and your parents still help him after what he did?"

Katya gives me a stricken look, then presses her lips together. "I'm still his friend because I've known him most of my life," she says, "and I want desperately to believe there's some way to justify what he did because I *can't* believe the Alexi Rey I knew would do that. He knows how angry I am, I promise you. And as for helping him, no. I can't speak for my parents, but I've told him *I* will have no part in his war." She gestures to me. "Except for this. I'll facilitate peace. Anything to end this before we're all destroyed."

"Katya, this isn't about peace," I tell her. "I'm here because he took Max."

"He knows how I feel about *that*, too," she says.

The parlor is empty, apart from a young man who sits unobtrusively on the windowsill. I remember him from Katya's wedding. "Prince Dimitri," I say, using his new title.

"Princess Esmae." He darts a look at Katya. "Everything okay, love?"

She nods. "Where is he?"

"He's five minutes away. Can I get you a drink, Esmae?"

"I'm fine, thank you."

"What a lovely, awkward conversation," *Titania* huffs in my ear. "My favorite kind. Can't you make it more interesting?"

I resist the urge to deactivate my earpiece. Instead, I just ignore her. This makes her start singing, a pirate's song about buried treasure, with a lot of bawdy lyrics that would be unspeakably funny coming from *Titania* if I wasn't on edge. "Stop it," I hiss.

"I'm only trying to cheer you up!"

And now of course Katya and Dimitri are giving me strange looks because I appear to be talking to myself.

"You're not helping," I say.

"Who are you talking to?"

I freeze. That's *his* voice.

I turn. Alex is in the doorway. His brownish golden skin is paler than it was a few weeks ago, probably from a lack of sleep and constant injury. I wonder if I look the same. If I, too, have those dark shadows under my eyes. If I, too, have scrapes and bruises all over me.

His eyes, exactly like mine, stare at me with so much *feeling* that I can't bear to look. So I turn away and address Katya and Dimitri. "Can I speak to my brother alone? I give you my word I won't kill him."

It's a dark attempt at a joke, but they obviously don't take it as such. Well, who can blame them? *I* probably wouldn't trust me.

But they do leave, shutting the parlor door gently behind them. I have no doubt guards are right outside, ready to burst in if either of us misbehaves.

I sit down, crossing one leg over the other and resting my forearms on the arms of the chair. The posture of royalty, cold and unyielding. He sits in the opposite chair, but doesn't opt for the same position. Instead, he draws one knee up to rest his chin on it. Like a vulnerable schoolboy. I want to throw something at him.

"You've been busy," he says.

I can tell he means King Yann. More specifically, framing *him* for the assassination of King Yann. "You're one to talk," I reply. "Is Max alive?"

"Yes. I swear."

I tilt my head, searching every shift in his body and every note in his voice for a lie. "Is he hurt?"

He has the good grace to look sheepish. "We had a fight. If it makes you feel better, he gave as good as he got." He gestures to the bruise on one cheek.

"Where is he?"

"You know I can't tell you that."

"Then tell me what it'll take to get him back."

Alex blinks. "You really care that much? About Max?"

"You don't have any idea who he really is," I say. "I'm surprised Kirrin hasn't told you. Actually, I'm *shocked* Kirrin hasn't told you. See, I always assumed he cared about Max, but if he did, why did he help you take him? If he really cared, why did he leave Max's life in the hands of the people who hate him most? Ask him if you don't believe me. Ask him why you were really exiled from Kali. Ask him why you're still alive."

From the expression on his face, I can tell I've thrown him. He doesn't know what to make of this, or of the implication that Kirrin has been keeping secrets from him. His hand clenches on his knee, but he only says, "Your surrender. That's what will get him back. I'll trade him for you."

"So you can finish that duel the way you really wanted to?"

"I don't want that." Alex's voice is tight and pained. "I never wanted that. There's a lot you don't know about that duel."

I stare at him, torn between an urge to hurt him and a desperate, treacherous need to *know*. "Then tell me," I say at last. "I'm here. I'm listening. Tell me what I don't know."

He opens his mouth, then closes it. He shakes his head, not meeting my eyes.

"I don't know why I bother," I say bitterly, "And for the record, no. I will not trade myself for Max."

"Do you care about him or not?" Alex asks, bewildered. "I can't tell if he cares about you. He wouldn't tell us anything. We promised him we'd let Elvar and Guinne live, that we'd let him live, that we'd even let you live, and he still wouldn't talk. We offered him the crown of Arcadia if he helped me get Kali back." At that, I laugh. Max knows exactly how much Arcadia is worth. "We threatened you. You know what he said? *Esmae can take care of herself.*"

"Well, she can," I say, inordinately pleased that Max refused to give in. "The Blue Knights won't sneak up on me twice, I assure you. Actually, that reminds me. Why am I still here? Why didn't they kill me?"

Alex's throat moves. "Maybe I don't want you dead."

"Do I need to remind you of the fact that Rama died because you killed him believing he was me?"

"I'm sorry. I am so, so sorry about that."

This is a different apology from the one he gave me right after duel. He was obviously shocked then, but his apology was hollow and insincere. This one is broken, scored deeply by guilt. When did this happen? When did he decide he was sorry?

"And Shloka?"

That startles him. "Shloka? The country?"

"Are you joking? You're really going to pretend you don't know?"

"Know what?"

"*This*," I snarl, standing up and unbuttoning my dress. Two buttons down, the skin just above my right breast is marked with a vivid red scar.

He stands too, eyes wide. He approaches me, one hand outstretched as if to touch the scar. He draws his hand back at the last moment. I frown at him. Why is he so surprised?

"Who did that to you?"

My temper snaps and I shove him hard in the chest. "You did! Your favorite general and her band of mercenaries ambushed me in Shloka and almost killed me."

"*Leila?*" he recoils. "No, she wouldn't. I never gave her permission to do that. I would *never* have allowed it."

"Did you give her permission to murder Maya Sura?" I ask softly.

Alex draws in a sharp breath.

"Yes," I say, "I know all about Arcadia."

"Maya Sura is dead?"

"Yes, he's dead. I saw him at her feet, murdered for no reason other than that he knew too much. And if Leila Saka didn't do that on *your* orders, whose orders were they? Who thinks they can tell your general what to do? Or does your general think she can do what she wants?"

Alex's jaw works. He turns away and sinks back into his chair, his head buried in his hands. I suppose, if someone were to paint him now, he'd make a romantic picture. The handsome, golden hero, at his lowest before he rises once more to glory. That's how they'll tell it. And the next picture will have him shining in battle, and then the last in the sequence will show him with a crown on his head. That's the way of the world. The dark fall, the golden rise.

"The very first thing you learn on Kali is respect for your elders," Alex says unexpectedly, raising his head slowly. "How can you learn if you don't respect your teachers? How can you grow well if you don't respect your family? All that. I've been good at it. I've been a good son, a good student."

"Yes, I noticed."

"But," he adds quietly, "I think those who came before us created a world we were doomed to fail in. Haven't you noticed it's you and me at the heart of this war while our elders stand at the periphery?"

I shrug. "It's our war."

"Is it? I'm not saying we shouldn't accept responsibility for what we've done, but the deck was stacked against us from the start. This war was inevitable because of choices other people made before we were even born. Grandmother cursed our mother because of Queen Vanya's death, so Mother sent you away. We grew up apart and now look where we are. Meanwhile, Grandmother is a minor player in our story and goes on as if nothing happened."

"She tried to stop the war."

"Too little, too late. What about Rickard and all his promises? What about Elvar? What about Kirrin and Amba? What about Queen Vanya, who chose our father as her heir instead of Elvar? Where would we be without all those choices?"

"What about *your* choices?" I demand. "You could have made a different choice in that duel, but you didn't. The consequences of that are on *you*. You're right. We were born into a world where the deck was already stacked against us, a world with the echoes of hundreds of choices the generations before us made. But you've played your part, too, Alex."

He looks up at me, standing in front of him, and rises. "What do you want from this war?"

"I want you to hurt the way I hurt," I say. "You took my best friend from me. You lied to me. I loved you and you broke my heart. So I want you to feel all of that. I want you to know what it is to be broken. I want to take away your reputation, your glory, and your crown. I want you to *hurt*."

There are tears on my face when I'm finished, and on his too. "You will be the end of me," he says.

"Yes."

"The duel was supposed to prevent that from happening, but it *made* it happen."

"Fate is a trickster god, Alex. You should have used your free will and ignored it. You should have chosen differently."

"I did. I tried." And then: "I did love you, you know. I *do* love you. You're my sister."

I smile a little. "But?"

"But you won't stop, will you?"

"You know the answer to that. My glorious, golden brother. Do you remember when we first met after the competition, when you told me I was no one? You were so proud then, so angry someone had actually beaten *you*, so sure of who you were."

"That boy is gone," he says. "I'm not sure of much anymore. I hurt more than you can possibly know."

"Give Max back, Alex."

"I can't do that. Not unless you stop. You'll be the end of me if you don't stop. Or I'll be the end of you." His voice cracks at that part, as if he hasn't already been the end of me once. As if it hurts. "Esmae, *please*. You can still stop. Don't make me fight you. Don't make this worse. It's not too late."

The plea doesn't move me. Rama never got a chance to plead. I never got a chance to plead.

"This will destroy our family," he goes on. "It'll destroy our House. Centuries of kings and queens, all gone."

I think of the long, grand gallery of beautiful portraits on Kali, all those faces lined up on the walls. All those ghosts.

"Maybe it's time the great House of Rey came to an end," I reply. "After all, what are we now? A broken House, a ruined House. A House of rage and sorrow."

Alex opens his mouth, but he doesn't get to speak. The door slams open unexpectedly, startling us.

Princess Katya runs back in. "Bear's in trouble!" she cries.

"How can Bear be in trouble?" Alex asks. "He's in Arcadia."

"No, he's not. He's on Kali."

"*What?*"

"How is that possible?" I demand. "How did he get there?"

"Lord Selwyn invited him there for a game of dice. I assume in retaliation for Max. I don't know what the stakes were, but Bear obviously couldn't resist." Distress colors Katya's voice. "You know how badly he wants this war to end before either of you are killed."

All the blood has leeched out of Alex's face. He and Katya look at me, as if I somehow have fairytale powers and can conjure Bear out of thin air.

"I'll get him back," I snap and storm out.

As I rush out of the palace and into Blackforest, Winter's capital city, I unmute *Titania*. Incredibly, she's still singing.

"*Titania*, stop! We need to get back to Kali."

"Why?" she asks.

"Lord Selwyn did what he does best. He tricked Bear into a game of dice, and I dread to think what the stakes could be."

No matter which side he and I are on, I love Bear, in the simple, total way I loved Rama. If Lord Selwyn touches so much as one hair on his—

"What are you going to do?" *Titania* asks anxiously.

"I don't know. Elvar and Guinne won't let go of Bear easily, not with Max still gone."

"Esmae."

I falter, arrested by the way she said my name. "What is it?"

"I think I might know a way you can save Bear." It's a very imprecise, human sentence. This is not a sentient spaceship sharing data. This is a friend trying to find some way to avoid telling me an ugly truth. The back of my neck crawls with dread. "There's something you need to know."

CHAPTER TWENTY-TWO

My heart feels cold, like there's nothing left there. Maybe it's shock. I stand in the balcony above the Throne Hall, the scene of the game of dice, and watch the figures below. Elvar, Guinne, Selwyn, royal guards, courtiers. And on the other side, Bear. Alone.

He's dead. That was what *Titania* told me. She has a connection to Amba and Kirrin, which is news to me, and it lets her sometimes see the things *they* see. *He's dead.* A prisoner in a woodcutter's cottage, hidden away, shielded and guarded. *He's dead.* It was what she had wanted to tell me the morning after the Lotus Festival, but she'd kept quiet after Max had been taken. She had felt it would be too cruel to tell me at such a time.

Below me, Bear's face is flushed with shame and fury. "Another round," he says, and then grinds out, "Please."

Lord Selwyn smiles. "Is that wise? You've already gambled and lost your mother's wedding ring, your freedom, *and* your claim to the throne if the twins die. What else can you possibly stake?"

"Max?"

"You've already told us you have no control over what your brother does with Max," Lord Selwyn replies, "so that's not an honest stake. Come now, Prince Abra. End this humiliation before you make everything worse."

"You cheated."

"That's the response of a sore loser."

Bear's shoulders slump. "So what now? You lock me up until the war is over?"

"That about sums it up, yes. Have no fear, we'll make sure you're comfortable. Your uncle is kinder than I am. He insists that you be treated well."

Bear glares across at Elvar as if he finds this hard to believe, but I don't. I know Elvar carries around more guilt about what he's done than he lets on. He grips the arms of the throne very tightly now and says, "Bear, please. We can forget about this whole game and you can go back to Arcadia if you simply tell us where Max is."

"I can't help you, Uncle," Bear says, jaw clenched. "I was an idiot to let this get this far, but at least I've only gambled away what's mine. I can't betray Alex and give Max up. And," he adds, with a flash of his temper, "I don't want to give Max up anyway. He sent us into *exile*. He can stay where he is forever."

"He's my son!"

"Yes, the apple didn't fall far from the tree," Bear snaps back.

The clash of these two tempers won't end well.

But, instead of exploding, Elvar only rubs a tired hand over his face and blindfold. After a moment, he says, "Selwyn, send the wedding ring back to Kyra. You may have won it from the boy, but it doesn't sit right with me that the ring Cassel gave Kyra should be away from her."

"She gave it to me," Bear mutters.

"I don't doubt that. But if *you* can't have it, I think she'd prefer it returned to her."

Bear doesn't reply. He looks sullen, young and ashamed. My heart goes out to him, this boy who risked everything and came here to protect his family. I don't know what Lord Selwyn tempted him with, but I can guess: Elvar's total surrender of the crown back to Alex and the end of the war. Nothing else could have tempted Bear here, nothing except the irresistible possibility that he might have been able to save his brother and sister before they killed each other.

And of course Lord Selwyn cheated. There was never any chance he would have let Bear win.

"Take him away," Lord Selwyn says to the royal guards. Among them are Jemsy, Henry, and Juniper, who look unhappy about the whole thing. They know how I feel about Bear. They know how *Max* feels about Bear.

It's time to speak up.

"Do you think Max would be happy about this?" I ask, my voice ringing through the Hall.

Heads jerk up to the balcony. Bear's face brightens, while Lord Selwyn's does exactly the opposite.

"Max would understand," Lord Selwyn says.

"No, he wouldn't." I march down the spiral steps and join them in the main chamber of the Hall. "He loves Bear. Alex and Bear are more his brothers than they were ever mine." Both Bear and Lord Selwyn react with shock to this, but I cock my head at the latter. "Didn't you ever wonder why all those attempts on their lives kept failing?"

"Esmae, what are you talking about?" Guinne asks, her brow creased with anxiety. "Have you seen Max? Is he safe?"

"He's alive," I say and turn back to Lord Selwyn. "You see now, don't you? Your own nephew kept them alive in spite of your best efforts to the contrary. So no, he wouldn't have understood. He would never have let you trick Bear into giving up his freedom. But you know all about tricks, don't you?"

"You'll have to stop speaking in riddles if you want me to understand you," he replies, eyes narrowed as he tries to anticipate what I'm about to do.

My heart doesn't feel so cold anymore. I miss the cold. As the pain rushes back, my voice cracks. "I know what you did!"

"If you mean my attempt to kill your brothers, the king understands I did that for *his* sake."

"Not that," I spit and turn abruptly to Bear. "Call Kirrin." "What? Me?"

"Well, he won't come if *I* call, will he?" I reply.

A shudder passes over the room, and then a cheerful voice behind me says, "You underestimate yourself, Esmae."

I turn, and there he is, the blue boy god with his mischievous eyes. He gives me a small, sweet smile. It's sincere. I've never doubted that Kirrin actually likes me. He just likes Alex more. His determination to bring about my end before I bring about my brother's is not personal. I don't trust him, but I don't really blame him either. I'd probably do the same if I were him.

Unease ripples across the crowd, including Elvar and Guinne. A god's presence makes this tricky, especially the presence of the god who has openly chosen the enemy's side. Kirrin takes in the room, eyebrows raised. "Well, this is certainly interesting. Good day to you, King Elvar, Queen Guinne." He turns back to me. "If you called me here to rescue Bear, Alex already asked and I'll tell you what I told him. I can't. My hands are tied."

"No one's asking you to risk your godhood," I say, irritated. Both Amba and Kirrin fall back on this refrain whenever it's convenient. "I just need you to speak. No one in this room will doubt your word."

"And what is it you want me to say?"

My voice isn't quite steady as I say, "Tell them what you found in the woodcutter's cottage."

Bear flinches. Kirrin frowns. "How do you know about that?"

"Tell them."

"I don't take well to mortals giving me commands," Kirrin says, but he sounds more amused than offended.

"And I don't take well to gods who go out of their way to plot my death," I reply, "but here we are."

"You are a thorn in my side," he says but turns to Elvar and Guinne. "Alexi and Bear went to the woodcutter's cottage to rescue a prisoner. One of their spies had spotted the prisoner briefly on a scouting trip and had rushed back to report what she'd seen, so we went to see for ourselves. We got past the guards, past the shield, and went inside. The prisoner was dead. Only just. I assume whoever imprisoned him found out we were coming and had him killed before we could rescue him."

Elvar looks completely baffled. "But what does this have to do with any of us?"

140

"Who was he?" I ask, teeth cold and clenched. "Who was the prisoner, Kirrin?"

There's an unbearable kindness in Kirrin's face as he says, "Cassel."

The effect of that name on the room is cataclysmic. Bear makes a sound that can only be a sob. The courtiers reel. Elvar staggers up from his chair. "What?"

"It was your brother. The former king of Kali." Kirrin jerks his head at Bear and me. "Their father."

Their father. I want the cold back. I want it to stop hurting.

"Impossible," Guinne says, her voice trembling. "Cassel died almost twelve years ago. We mourned him. He had a king's funeral. We all saw him!"

"There's no way to know for sure what you saw," Kirrin says. "Perhaps he was injected with a stasis serum and, once the funeral was over, his captor retrieved him? I cannot say. What I can tell you is that the man we found was unquestionably Cassel. He has been alive all these years, imprisoned in that cottage. He died a week ago."

Tears flow freely down Elvar's cheeks, soaking his blindfold. "It cannot be true," he croaks.

"It's true," Bear says, his voice broken on a sob. "We couldn't believe it when our spy came back claiming she had seen him, but we had to find out. We went to get him. We wanted our father back. And we hoped, if we got him back—" he stops, unable to continue.

"He would have been king," Elvar finishes for him. "The war would have been over."

"We wanted to come home. We wanted him back." Bear looks at me, his eyes wet. "We hoped you'd forgive Alex. We would have been a family, all of us together for the first time."

"But it was not to be," says Kirrin quietly. "I am sorry. Truly. There was no saving him."

Like two sides of a mirror, Elvar and Bear both weep, united by the only thing they have in common. The war *would* have ended. If there is one thing I know, it's that Elvar loved his brother more than almost anything else in the world. He would have handed back the crown, begged my father's forgiveness, and Kali would have been in one piece once more. And would I have forgiven Alex? Would I have been able to move on from what he did to Rama, to me? I don't know, but there was a *chance*. Perhaps my father could have healed a rift no one else could. Perhaps. Is that why this hurts so much? There was a chance, but now we'll never know.

I don't cry. I wait. And the whole time, I never take my eyes off the man who did this.

"Who did it?" Elvar asks, his voice trembling with anger. "Who took him from us? Who murdered him when their secret was exposed?"

"We cannot be certain," Kirrin says carefully, but he follows my gaze to Lord Selwyn.

Selwyn blanches. "That is a terrible accusation."

"No one accused you," Kirrin says calmly. "You're oddly quick to defend yourself, Lord Selwyn."

"Of course it was him," Bear bursts out. "Who else could it have been? You're the *only* person who wanted my father out of the way!"

"That's not true," Guinne says, getting up, "Selwyn has much to answer for, but he would never have had Cassel killed."

But Elvar's voice booms across the Hall, as sudden as thunder. "You told me it was a good thing he was gone," he growls at Selwyn, who takes a step back. "You told me I could finally come out of his shadow and prove myself."

"I said that, yes, but I didn't take him." Selwyn's panicking now. His lies aren't working on the king he's manipulated for years. "Elvar, please. You can't truly believe I would do such a thing."

"You wanted me to execute them!" Elvar points in Bear's direction. "You told me to kill two *children* to stop them ever taking my throne away. And if it hadn't been for Max, I would have let you persuade me. I would have let them die." Elvar's face is almost deathly white. "After that, why wouldn't I believe you would do such a thing?"

"I swear to you, I did not. I swear it on my life, on Max's life. I swear it on Guinne's life!"

"Don't you *dare*," Elvar roars. "You will be executed for treason."

I will never waste any grief on Lord Selwyn, not after everything he's done, but this is too fast. Before I can open my mouth, Guinne reaches for Elvar, her normally sure, graceful movements replaced by panic. "Elvar, please. Please just *listen*. I know Cassel's murder must be punished, but this is not the way to do it. Hold a trial, gather evidence, and then decide. The evidence will show Selwyn didn't do it." She sounds so sure. She has so much faith in him. She really doesn't have any idea what he is.

"He won't be given a chance to slither away," Elvar says. "He will be executed. My word is final."

All the blood drains out of Lord Selwyn's face. He puts his hands on Elvar's shoulders, clutching him. "Please," he begs. "Please. I swear to you, Elvar, I never touched Cassel. Don't do this."

"My brother is dead," Elvar says, tears on his face. Two royal guards approach to pull Selwyn off him, but Selwyn won't let go. "My brother is *dead*."

"Elvar, please—"

"Take a moment to think, please—"

"I didn't, I swear—"

"Give him a chance—"

Selwyn and Guinne are both pleading, their voices crossing over the other's in panic and desperation. I watch them, expecting to feel only hatred because of what he did to my father, but I'm surprised that instead I feel something else: doubt.

That *look* in his eyes.

I open my mouth—

—and Elvar reaches out to Selwyn, and snaps his neck.

An instant, and it's over. Elvar was once a formidable warrior. Selwyn never stood a chance.

Courtiers cry out. Bear gasps. And as Selwyn crumples to the floor, Guinne goes with him, keening. "No, no, no, no, no," she cries, and I can't help thinking it's almost exactly the way I knelt over Rama and cried *no, no, no, no*.

Shock holds me frozen for a split second, but then as chaos breaks out in the Hall and the rest of the royal guards rush in to make sure Elvar is safe, I move. I rush to Bear, abandoned by the guards who had been tasked with keeping him in line, and grab his wrist. "This is your only chance to get out," I whisper. "Come on."

Trained in war from the moment of his birth, he recovers faster than I do and immediately follows me back up the spiral steps to the balcony. I lead him out of the little door there to the servant's corridor outside the Hall and we run from there to the nearest stairway up to the roof. There, tucked away among chimneys and hidden by the shadow of the spiky towers nearby, is *Titania*.

I push Bear toward her. "She'll take you back to Winter."

"Come with me," he says.

"You know I can't. Go!"

"Wait." He grabs my hand, as if afraid that he'll lose me for good if he lets go. "Is it true? Would Elvar have had us executed if Max hadn't convinced him to exile us instead?"

"Yes." I squeeze his hand, then gently pull away. "You need to go before they remember you're supposed to be our prisoner. Kirrin can tell you all about Max."

"He's on the Empty Moon," Bear blurts.

"What?"

"Max. He's being held in Kirrin's palace on the Empty Moon." Bear flushes, no doubt feeling guilty for giving away Alexi's secrets. "That place, it does things to you."

"What do you mean, it *does* things? What things?"

"I don't know. Kirrin says it depends on the person. Some people never want to leave. Some people forget who they are. Some people leave and never feel whole again. And that's just the ones who survive the seas," he adds, biting his lip. "Our mother lost her hand in those seas. She was lucky. Mortals aren't supposed to stay there long. We can't cope with so much celestial power."

"Why would Kirrin do that to Max? He always seemed to care about him. Why would he risk something terrible happening to him there?"

Bear bites his lip, then mumbles, "Because they think you'll get to him in time. They want you to know he's there. They *want* you to go get him."

"But that makes no sense," I protest. "Why bother imprisoning him there just to get *me* to go there?"

"Kirrin said it was the only way to get you there, to use Max to lure you," Bear says. He rubs the back of his neck. "You know I shouldn't be telling you all this, but if Max really did save us, he doesn't deserve this. I don't know what will happen to him. He needs to get out of there before it's too late. But *you* can't go. It's not safe. Only gods and celestial creatures have power there."

Only gods and celestial—

"Amba," I say, as the truth hits me. "They want me to go there because only a god will be able to get me into that palace. They want me so desperate that I call her for help. And when I do, when she comes, Kirrin will release Sorsha."

Bear nods unhappily. "I'm sorry."

They want you to come after me. That was the last thing Max said to me. He knows how Kirrin thinks. Did he guess this was why they came for him?

"Go," I say to Bear, giving him a gentle push. "You need to get out of here."

He gives me a quick, hard hug and then runs across the carved roof stone to the ship. Right before he reaches *Titania*'s open hatch, I see him falter. He looks over Erys, the spiky skyline, the forests, the dome of the university. *Home*. That's what he's thinking. It's the home he wants so badly, and now he has to flee from it.

Then he vanishes inside the ship and is gone.

CHAPTER TWENTY-THREE

Titania

The boy is afraid of me. He sits awkwardly in one of the seats in my control room and toys with a band of knotted, colored cord that has been wrapped around his wrist. Occasionally, he looks up and darts nervous glances around him. After twenty minutes of this, I've had it.

"I don't bite," I sniff.

He startles. "Sorry. Um, I'm Bear."

"I know." And then, just for the fun of it, I put on a grim voice. "I know all about you, Abra Rey."

He pales, an expression so priceless that I let out a peal of laughter. He's stunned for a moment, and then a sheepish grin lights up his face. "Esmae always says you're a handful," he tells me. "I get it now."

"*You're* a handful," I snipe.

"How old are you, six?"

"Thirteen, actually," I say primly, "And also thousands of years old, depending on how you look at it."

He smiles, but it's a little wobbly. I've learned to recognize what a smile like that means on a human face. It means they're only temporarily amused by what they hear because they are unhappy and they won't be distracted from whatever it is that made them unhappy.

I hazard a guess. "You mourn your father."

"It's pretty brutal to lose a father twice," he says, "Especially when you don't remember the first time very well."

I analyze the rhythm of his voice, the pitch of each inflection. "But that's not what you're unhappy about right now," I deduce.

"How do you know that?"

"Data."

He blinks, but accepts that without further questions. After a moment, he speaks, so quietly I'm not sure I would have been able to hear him if I had been human. "I don't know how to save them both."

"You can't," I tell him, "but if it helps, know that they both love you very much."

He looks out of my glass windows, and I see the stars sparkle in his tears.

I know, I want to say. *I'm afraid too.*

I take him back to Winter. As I return to Kali, to that glittering jewel in the sky, I wonder what will become of that boy by the time this is all over.

It takes hours for the palace to calm down after Lord Selwyn's execution. Or, rather, from the revelation that a beloved former king was held prisoner for years only to be murdered before he could be rescued. The war council is in uproar, the servants are in shock, and the royal family is in pieces. On one screen, I see the dot that represents Queen Guinne retreat alone to her suite. On another, I see the dot that represents Rickard travel painfully slowly from his own rooms to the conservatory, where King Elvar has gone to pray at the gods' altar.

And I hear Esmae in the war room with the rest of the war council, telling them where Max is. I hear their reaction.

"The Empty Moon?" That's the old queen Cassela. "Are you certain?"

"It makes sense."

"Then he's lost to us," she says, her voice heavy with sadness.

I hear Esmae's sharp intake of breath before she speaks. "What do you mean, he's lost to us? Someone needs to go get him!"

"I would dearly love to have Max back, but you cannot seriously expect anyone to brave the Empty Moon! Need I remind you that your mother lost her hand there? She was lucky to leave with her life. And that was when Kirrin wasn't working against us! How do you expect someone from our side to survive a rescue mission into the heart of a hostile god's territory?"

"Kirrin *wants* Max to be rescued! That's part of this game. He wouldn't make it impossible."

"You said yourself that he wants you to have to call on Amba for help, which we all know would be catastrophic. That makes it impossible."

"The Hundred and One can go," Sybilla snaps. "We'd gladly take that risk for Max."

"No," Esmae says. Inadvertently, Sybilla has hit her weakness. It was easy for Esmae to talk about sending seasoned warriors from Kali's legions to the Empty Moon, but the moment she started to picture the Hundred and One there, those children she has been training for months, her resolve broke. There's a tremor in her voice. "She's right. It's not fair to send anyone."

A little while later, I feel her clamber across my wing. I open my hatch and she drops into the control room. Pale and bruised, she looks very small and young all of a sudden.

"I hate them," she says, fists clenched at her sides. "I hate them all." I don't know if she means Alexi and Kirrin, or the war council, or her entire family, or all of the above. I don't ask. "Everything's slipping away. Rama's gone, Rickard is a ruin, I've lost my father. I don't even have Amba. Even at her worst, she was still *there*."

"And now Max," I say.

"*Lost to us*," she repeats bitterly.

"You can do this on your own. We can fly there and see how far we can get. You can refuse to call on Amba, no matter what. If there's no way to do it without her, turn back. At least you'll know."

She laughs a little and wipes a hand across her nose. "He's been there for days. Who knows what's happened to him?"

"Then we'd better hurry."

"*Titania*, I can't. What if I have no choice but to call for her? Sorsha will be free. And the first thing they'll do is send her after *you*."

I don't know how to process that. I am a machine, a weapon to be wielded. I am not supposed to be protected. *Loved*.

I cannot cry, but I think I understand why mortals do.

"I want to show you something," I tell her.

She turns in surprise as I project a recording into the middle of the room. A second version of Esmae appears in slightly translucent holographic form, silent and still inside a glass pod while small, delicate robotic tools work on her wounds. Max stands beside the pod, one hand on the outside of the glass.

"What is this?" Esmae asks, taken aback.

"*Shhh*. Listen."

There's a crackle as I adjust the volume, and then we hear Max's voice. "What can you see?" he asks the silent, wounded Esmae in the pod. "The journey to the celestial heavens is a cold walk across a bridge of stars. At the end, all the way across, you can probably see someone waiting for you. Maybe it's your father. Maybe it's Rama. I don't know. I just know how easy it is to keep walking. This is the secret no one tells," he adds, his voice raw. "It's easy to go. It's harder to stay. The hardest thing is to live, but it's worth every minute of the battle. You know that. I know you know that. That's why you fight, that's why you're fighting right now. And if anyone can win this fight, it's you. So don't go. Stay. Come back to me."

He keeps talking to her, for hours. I remember he didn't leave her side that entire journey back to Kali. He tells her about a jealous, lonely child who made his own family out of a hundred other jealous, lonely children. He talks to her about his first battle, against a group of mercenaries who had been sent by King Cassel's greedy cousin to kidnap his two children, and how they had to take Max too because he wouldn't let go of them. He tells her the first thought he had when he saw her picking up the bow and arrow on the day of the competition: *She's so alone.*

In the end, he says, "I've loved you since the day you first looked at the bitter, broken things I'd made in my tower. You *looked*. No one had ever bothered to before." He presses his hand harder against the glass. "Come back. Please come back."

Then it's over. He's gone. Esmae reaches out a hand as if she wants to bring him back, and then her hand drops. "Why did you show me that?" she asks.

"Because I know you want him back," I tell her, "so I'm giving you a push."

CHAPTER TWENTY-FOUR

I don't take much. A long, hooded jacket to put on over my war gear if it gets cold, basic supplies in a rucksack, the Black Bow. *Titania* has arrows, other weapons, and more supplies on board already, so I don't waste time getting anything else. The quicker I can get out of the palace, the less likely anyone will realize what I'm doing and try to stop me.

But when I open my suite door to leave, I find Elvar outside.

I freeze. It's a little after midnight; he's the last person I expected to run into at such a time. My uncle looks older and grayer than he did yesterday, but he has a rueful smile on his face. I know he can hear the clink of metal in my rucksack.

"You're going to get him," he says. It's not a question.

"Yes."

"Here." He hands me a thin, sheathed object.

I take it. The sheath is supple and smooth, but underneath I can feel the deft, liquid lightness of truly spectacular steel. "What is it?"

"Cassel's sword." A brief, wistful look crosses Elvar's face. "*Lullaby*, he called it. I wanted him to give it a more traditional, powerful name, but he refused. It was so sharp, he said, that it would always be a quick, merciful end for whoever he had to use it against. He said it was a kind way to sing people to sleep."

"*Lullaby*," I repeat it, little more than a whisper. My father's sword. I didn't even know it existed.

"When we thought Cassel was dead all those years ago, I took the sword. It should really have been given to one of his children, but I was selfish. I wanted to keep any part of him I could. It's yours now. My brave, kind girl." Elvar puts a hand briefly on my cheek, then turns away. "Good luck."

I watch him go, then slip away in the opposite direction. I take a stairway into one of the spiky towers of the palace, up to a balcony. *Titania* hovers in the air on the other side of the balcony.

And standing at the balustrade, her arms crossed over her chest, is Sybilla.

"Don't make this a fight," I say.

"That depends," she replies. She tosses her braid over her shoulder and climbs nimbly over the balustrade onto *Titania*'s wing. "On whether or not you're going to try to keep me from coming with you."

"You know you could die on the Empty Moon, right?"

"So?" she says. "I don't want to hear it. Max is my family. So are you. Let's go."

"What about Radha? Who's going to keep her safe if we're both gone?"

"No need to worry about that," Radha says from behind me. I swivel around and see she's dressed for travel, her beautiful dresses swapped for thick leggings, a tunic, a jacket and sturdy boots. She smiles at me.

Sybilla is appalled. "*You* can't come!"

"I can and I will," Radha replies calmly. "We all go, or none of us go."

"That's ridiculous," Sybilla snaps. Her tone is even more aggressive than usual. "What good are *you* going to be? You may have been trained to stab a man with a sewing needle, but that won't be much use on the Empty Moon. You should stay."

Hurt flashes across Radha's face, but her voice is steel when she replies. "Oh, I'm so sorry," she says, "I didn't realize I had to be *useful* to be your friend." With deliberate movements, she climbs over the balustrade and steps hard onto the wing on the other side. She wobbles a little, her balance off, but she keeps going. "No, I can't fight like the two of you can. I'm not fast or strong or whatever's important to you. In spite of all that, I'm coming and I dare you to try and stop me."

Sybilla's mouth opens and closes several times. Then she snaps it shut for a final time, turns on her heel, and storms off to the open hatch.

Radha looks at me. "She *really* doesn't like me, does she?"

"You'll have to talk to Sybilla if you want to know how she feels about you," I say and go over the balustrade myself. "Come on. We need to get out of here before my great-grandmother realizes what I'm up to and orders the shields sealed to stop me."

Radha follows me to the hatch and drops down after me. *Titania* seals it shut, waits until we're strapped into our seats, and takes off at once. "This is fun!" she chirps at us. "We can play travel games!"

"I *love* travel games," Radha says happily.

"Of course you do," Sybilla mutters.

"What was that?"

"Nothing." Sybilla waits until we've crossed Kali's shields and *Titania* has leveled out in open space. "I need a drink. I'll be in the galley if anyone needs me."

She marches away, bootstrikes hard and angry. *Titania* huffs. "That girl is terrible for my floors," she complains.

I get out of my seat, too. "I have some repairs to do."

When I climb down into *Titania*'s engine room, I pick up the tools and tighten nuts that aren't even loose, hammer in bolts that are already secure, and oil the mechanics. It's noisy in the engine room and the smell of fuel stings my nose, but I like it. As a child, the smell of spaceship fuel reminded me of wing war lessons with Rickard and the dream of home.

I needed to not be up there. These tasks aren't necessary, but they're keeping me busy. There's a procedure for maintaining *Titania*'s mechanics, a specific order that has to be followed so that I don't end up burning myself or getting caught in a whirring blade, and focusing on that checklist means there's not much room to think about other things. Like my dead friend or my dead father. Like why Alex was upset when he found out General Saka tried to kill me. Like how I'm supposed to cross the Empty Moon and get Max back without losing Sybilla or Radha along the way. Like the growing tally of people I've killed. Like the whisper at the back of my mind that thinks of that look on Lord Selwyn's face before he died and wonders if maybe he didn't imprison and murder my father after all.

Those are all things I can't stop to think too much about. *Stop too long, and you'll never go on.* Amba used to say that.

My mind is full of thorns.

Miles and miles of impossibly beautiful stars, moons, and wormholes later, I feel a lurch beneath my feet. I return to the upper deck and meet Sybilla in the corridor, a mostly empty bottle of plum wine in her hand.

"Are we there?" I ask *Titania* when we're back in the control room.

"Almost," she says. "I'd buckle up if I were you."

I've only just buckled myself into my seat when a jagged, icy blue rock appears in the distance.

Radha takes a deep, awed breath. "The Empty Moon."

The pale, almost translucent moon grows larger as we get closer, viciously sharp and mercilessly blue. I think about how Max and I saw it a few months ago, from right about where we are now, and it's all I can do not to turn my head to look for him beside me.

"Here we go," *Titania* says.

As we dip toward the Empty Moon, I notice something.

"The song," I say. "I can't hear it."

"What song?" Sybilla asks, confused.

"When Max and I were here last time, we could hear the wolves of the Empty Moon," I tell them. "They were *singing*. We could hear them from all the way up here. I don't know how, but we could." It was as eerie as it was beautiful. "And now I can't hear anything."

"The hounds of the Empty Moon have been singing for a hundred years," *Titania* says. "The song is their lament. It's how they mourn Valin, their fallen god."

Radha gives me a worried look. "Maybe they're not singing because they're not here anymore. Didn't you say Kirrin might use them against us in battle? What if he's taken them to join Alexi?"

I nod. "It's possible. General Khay has been expecting it for some time."

"Well," says Sybilla, "Wolves or no wolves, we have a prince to rescue. Let's get down there."

"*Titania*, see if you can find Kirrin's palace."

Titania swoops lower until she crosses the moon's shields with a judder. Once she's about a hundred feet or so above the surface of the Empty Moon's dark, cold blue seas, she scans our surroundings. We watch on the monitor as a map slowly takes shape, mainly sea broken by white stony beaches and islands with ice forests, and then, eventually, the outline of a palace in the distance.

"There," I say, but I know it's not going to be as simple as that. "I don't think you'll be able to fly there, but it's worth a try."

Titania heads for the palace, but then she's pulled in the opposite direction. Like gravity, the invisible force is irresistible and the ship judders dangerously as she tries to fight it. She probably could have beaten it anywhere else, but here, on a god's realm, it's too powerful for her.

"Hold tight!" she shrieks.

We do, but it doesn't do much good. Like an elastic band pulled too far, we snap back toward the moon's surface. I catch a glimpse of the white pebbled shore below us before we crash unceremoniously into it.

CHAPTER TWENTY-FIVE

I stagger out of the open hatch and onto the hard beach. Radha follows me out and is immediately sick on the stones. Sybilla holds her hair out of the way. I take deep, gulping breaths of ice and sea salt, squinting against cold white sunlight.

"*Titania*, are you okay?" I ask.

"My pride is somewhat bruised," she grumbles. "The rest of me is not."

"I'm going to take a wild stab in the dark," Sybilla says sarcastically, "And assume *Titania* isn't allowed to take us any further?"

"That is correct," says an unfamiliar voice.

I freeze. Sybilla and Radha look over my shoulder, eyes impossibly round. I turn cautiously to face the new arrival.

"Oh," I breathe. "You're a garuda."

The stranger towers above us, taller than any mortal I've ever seen. They have a human head, with brown skin, close shaved black hair, a hard jaw and sharp, delicate cheekbones. Below their brown neck is a torso covered in white feathers. Enormous, powerful white wings stretch out behind them. They have human legs, bare feet and a pair of ripped trousers hanging low on feathered hips.

"Yes," they say, "I am a garuda. My name is Vahana, and I am the guardian of the Empty Moon."

Sybilla snaps her astonished mouth closed. Radha's eyes stay wide, but she tentatively says, "We've been told Max Rey is in Kirrin's palace. We've come to take him home."

"You may do so," says Vahana, "if you can reach him. Your ship may not take you any further. She must wait here. To get to the palace, you must cross this sea and make your way through the ice forest. The palace is on the other side of the forest."

"Do we have to *swim* there?" Sybilla asks.

A flicker of a smile passes over Vahana's face. "You may use a boat," they say, and point behind us. I turn to see a boat waiting at the edge of the sea that I'm positive wasn't there before.

"And the tests?" I ask warily. "My brother told me there would be tests."

"There used to be three, but that was a different time. Now there is only one. You must survive the sea, the forest, and the test to gain entry to the palace. Very few mortals have ever been able to do so."

"What kind of test is it?"

"Truth," says Vahana. "There are truths in each of us that we do not dare look at, lest they break us. To pass the test, you will have to confront your truth."

Cold settles in my heart. Sybilla, Radha, and I look at each other. Sybilla looks more terrified than I've ever seen her.

"There is no shame in turning back," Vahana says.

I glare out at the unfriendly, churning sea. I can do this. *I won't let them win.* "I didn't come all this way to turn back now."

We collect our weapons and supplies, then we each put an earpiece in so that we can stay in contact with *Titania* and with one another if we get separated. I clamber into the boat first. Sybilla joins me and reaches for the oars, her jaw set. Radha wrings her hands in front of her, her face nakedly afraid, but she follows us without a word.

As we push off the shore, Vahana leaps into the air. Each of their wingbeats sends a gust of sharp, cold, salty air at us. "I will stay close to bear witness," they say. "Good luck."

They fly into the sky, vanishing into the bright white light. We watch them go, then Sybilla rows us further into the sea. She does this for half an hour and then I take my turn. By the time Radha takes hers, *Titania* has vanished with the shore. Her voice in my earpiece is crackly and keeps breaking up, like the moon itself doesn't want us to be able to speak to her.

"The sun is starting to go down," Sybilla says over the sound of Radha's ragged breathing. "I don't see the other shore. We might have to row right through the night."

I look warily into the water around us. It's cruel and eerie, viciously crashing against the sides of the boat, spraying salt and water so cold it burns. It's full of shadows and light, making it impossible to tell what's really under the surface. "Whoever isn't rowing can sleep," I say, "but we can't stop. The sooner we're back on land, the better."

"Are you sure about that?" Sybilla says darkly. "What if it's worse there?"

As the sun goes down, we continue to row in turns, eating small bites of dried meat and bread from our packs between each turn. The realities of being stuck on a boat start to sink in, too; there's no upside to having to empty your bladder into a water bottle, a feat that is easier said than done when you haven't got the ability to aim, but on top of that, Sybilla's monthly bleeding turns up a couple of hours into the evening and she spends ages searching for her menstrual cup by the light of only a sliver of a moon and a thousand stars before eventually finding it at the very bottom of her pack.

Some time before midnight, the others fall asleep. I keep rowing, my achy arms protesting every movement, and it's so cold that each breath creates a puff of white mist in front of me. I try to talk to *Titania*, but only a crackle answers me when I activate my earpiece. We're very much on our own.

The bump comes out of nowhere. One moment the boat is rocking normally on the water, the next it jerks violently to the side and almost flips over.

Sybilla jolts awake immediately. "What the hell was that?"

I grip my father's sword in both hands. "I don't know."

"Radha!" Sybilla barks over the roar of the sea. "Wake up!"

The boat jolts again. Radha stirs. As the third bump hits and the boat teeters all the way onto its side, I grab for her, but I'm too late. She tumbles over the side and into the water.

"Shit!" Sybilla cries as the boat rocks back onto its base. "Radha! Esmae, can you see her?"

Radha's head appears over the water and she gasps for air, thrashing wildly. We reach for her, scrambling to get hold of her arms, but she's too wet and slippery. She goes under again.

"Stay here," I say to Sybilla. She opens her mouth in furious protest, but I thrust the Black Bow and my father's sword at her and leap into the water before she can speak.

The shock of the cold makes me gasp and swallow a mouthful of seawater, which is strangely sweet, but I recover, take a gulp of air, and dive under the surface to find Radha.

It's dark below the surface, where the moonlight barely touches the water, and the only light is the eerie, otherworldly glow of flowers deep in the sea. *Blueflowers*. I use the glow of the flowers to find Radha, a shadow floundering desperately a few yards away.

I seize her arm. She looks into my eyes, her mouth wide open in a silent scream, and I look down to see she's fighting against a long, twisting shape pulling her deeper into the sea.

The creature rears its head to look at me and I see that it's like an eel, slippery and powerful, with horns and several rows of sharp white teeth. Terror freezes me in place, but only for an instant. With my chest aching from holding my breath and Radha's thrashing getting weaker, there's no time to waste on being afraid.

I slide my hands under the beast's slippery tail and try to pry it off Radha's ankle, but those teeth snap an inch away from my elbow. I pull my knife out of my boot and slash across the tail, spurting dark blood into the water. The creature's horned head lifts in a silent roar.

As I pull Radha free, the beast twists in the water and strikes. Teeth clamp into my shoulder, sending sharp white pain across every inch of my skin. I cry out and swallow seawater again, too much this time, and I choke.

In the middle of that searing, blinding white of the pain, I hear Max's voice. *This is the secret no one tells*, he says. *It's easy to go. It's harder to stay.*

I drive my knife into the beast's eye, forcing it to let me go, and Radha and I kick our way back to the surface.

Sybilla pulls us into the boat, then points a loaded crossbow into the water. As the horned head breaks the surface in pursuit, she fires. It sinks below the surface.

No one moves for a few seconds, waiting to see if the beast comes back. When nothing happens, Radha leans over the side of the boat to spit water. I let the blood and pain get the better of me and collapse into the bottom of the boat. Sybilla whirls around and tosses her crossbow into the corner with an angry *clang*.

"I *knew* you'd be a liability!" she snaps at Radha.

"Can this wait until later?" Radha demands. "Esmae's hurt!"

"Whose fault is that?"

"Mine! I know that! But now's not exactly the best time for this argument, is it?"

"*Enough*," I growl through the pain. "Someone help me get my tunic off."

With one arm hanging limply at my side, I can't do much but wriggle my body so they can get my tunic up and over my arms and head. With the tunic gone, the wound on my shoulder is exposed. Ragged flesh, teeth marks, a flash of white that looks sickeningly like bone.

Sybilla recoils, then searches frantically for the packs at the bottom of the boat. "I'll get the laser so we can seal the wound." I close my eyes and hear her shuffling and swearing for a moment or two before she says, "Esmae, I think your pack went overboard when the boat tipped. That's where the laser was."

"Of course," I groan. "How predictable. Do we have a needle and thread?"

"I do," Radha says.

"Okay, that'll do. I can sew the wound closed with my free hand if one of you helps me thread the needle."

"Don't be ridiculous," says Sybilla. "I'll do it."

"Can you even sew?" With medical lasers so readily available, no one is trained to sew wounds closed the old way anymore. But I grew up altering and mending my own clothes, so I think I can do a passable job on this wound.

"How hard can it be? Shove a needle in, loop it around the wound a few times, then tie off the thread. Easy!"

"Give me that needle," Radha says in exasperation, practically snatching it out of Sybilla's hands. She threads it expertly, even in the half dark. As she gets ready, Sybilla rips open a pack of sterile gauze and mops up the excess blood. Radha bites her lip as she looks down at me. "This is going to hurt, Esmae. I'm so sorry."

Sybilla wraps her arms around me, a gesture as much for comfort as it is to keep me from bucking and thrashing while Radha sews my wound closed. I squeeze my eyes shut and clench my teeth as the needle moves in and out, piercing the skin each time. Sybilla hums a song to drown out the terrible squelch of thread pulling ruined flesh back into place.

When it's over, they strip off the rest of my wet clothes, spread them out to dry on the floor of the boat, and put my dry jacket over me. Radha swaps her own wet clothes for the spare set she packed in her bag and huddles next to me so we can both keep warm.

Sybilla picks the oars back up, and we continue on.

CHAPTER TWENTY-SIX

I must have fallen asleep at some point, because I wake up with a start. The stars are still bright overhead and we've reached the shore.

Sybilla and Radha are on the beach next to the boat, taking stock of what we lost when the boat tipped. I test my shoulder. It hurts, but nothing's broken. My clothes are still damp, but I put them back on and shiver as I climb out of the boat and onto the beach. Snow and stones crunch under my boots.

"It should be colder," Sybilla says, shuddering.

"Speak for yourself. I think it's plenty cold, thanks."

"That's because you two got wet, but I stayed dry and I can only just feel the nip in the air. With all this snow and ice, it should be much colder than it is."

Beyond the beach is the dark line of the ice forest. The trees are bare, naked branches coated in sparkling frost, the ground covered in snow. Somewhere in the distance, past the trees, I can see one of the gleaming towers of Kirrin's palace. It glitters in the starlight, pale blue and trimmed with frost.

"Should we stay here until morning?" Radha asks. "Or risk the forest in the dark?"

"I'm not keen on staying near the water," says Sybilla, glancing back as if she expects to see another horned head come out of the sea at any moment.

"If we can see the palace from here, it can't be too far away," I say. "And the light from the moon and stars will reflect off all this snow, so we should be able to see better than we could when we were on the water. I think we should go ahead."

"Onwards, then," Sybilla says, shouldering her rucksack and drawing her sword out of its sheath at her hip. I hand Radha a knife. With my pack gone, I have only my sword, bow and a handful of arrows left, so I keep the first in my hand and the others hooked over my good shoulder.

We cross the beach and enter the line of naked trees, leaving the sea behind. The taste of sea salt on the air gives way to snow and sharp, spicy wood. The tower of the palace disappears as we walk deeper into the forest and the trees take over, so we use the stars to guide us the right way.

I walk slowly, my shoulder sending ripples of pain across my body each time I move. "I miss my blueflower," I say bitterly.

"Can't you ask Amba to give you another?" Radha asks.

"I don't think it works that way. There was power in that petal because it came from the flower my mother plucked."

Radha considers that, then says, "I envied you when we were little, you know. A goddess had sent you to the palace.

A goddess had *noticed* you. I wanted so badly to be noticed too." Her mouth lifts in a small, sad smile. "Now I see the trail of destruction the gods' favor has left around the very people they favor and I wonder if maybe I was lucky they never paid me any attention."

I open my mouth to agree but find I can't bring myself to say it. To say Amba's favor has brought me only ruin feels like a terrible betrayal.

"She told me stories," I hear myself say instead, into the snowy silence of the forest. "When I was alone and my world was still so small, she told me stories to make it bigger."

We walk on. Snow crunches under our feet and the trees cast sharp, cruel shadows across the starlit, white forest floor. Nothing stirs, not a branch, not a twig, not even a snowflake. It's a strange, eerie unreality, like we're picking our way across a dreamworld that will dissolve into smoke if we try to touch it. I realize we've seen snow and ice the whole time we've been on the Empty Moon, but not once has it actually *snowed*. Maybe the sky is not where this snow comes from. Maybe it's not even snow.

"Anyone feel any different?" Sybilla asks, obviously worried about the effect the moon might have on us.

"I don't think so," says Radha, and I shake my head, too. Of course, we've only been here half a day. Max has been here a *week*. I swallow. There's no way to know what's become of him.

An hour in, the wind picks up. Salt from the sea blows in, the first warning, and then the sparkling gusts of frost follow. At first it's just a wind, weaving in and out of the trees, but it doesn't die down. The sparkling frost turns into icy blue flurries, circling around us, and suddenly I can't see anymore. There's only the snow and the frost and the stars.

"Esmae!" Sybilla yells, sounding like she's very far away. "Radha!"

I can't see where I'm going, so I stand very still, grinding my feet into the forest floor. My hair whips against my cheeks and I squeeze my eyes shut.

Then, as quickly as it came, the wind is gone. The frost fades into nothing. The forest is still and silent once more.

And I'm alone.

"Sybilla!" I call, heart racing. "Where are you? Radha! Sybilla! Can you hear me?"

No answer. I call a few more times, but there's nothing. Not even the echo of my own voice. There are no footprints in the snow. No sign whatsoever they were ever even here.

The cruel, dark shadows of the trees loom over me. I don't know which way to go. I don't know how to find them.

Then there's the sound of snow crunching behind me. I spin around, so relieved—

—and see Rama.

His face breaks into a grin. "There you are," he says. "Do you have any idea how hard it's been to find you?"

"You're not real," I whisper.

"Thanks," he says drily. "That's nice. *Thank you for coming to find me, Rama. I'm sorry I keep demanding so much energy and activity from you, Rama. Would you like a nap, Rama?* All excellent options, but no! I get *you're not real.* Thanks, Ez."

I throw myself into his arms with a sob. He's so solid, and *warm.* I can feel the pulse in his throat against my cheek.

"Esmae," he groans, "I can't breathe."

I let him go, reluctantly, and he leans against a tree like it simply requires too much energy to stay on his own two feet any longer. I look up into his twinkling, dearly loved face. "You're so you," I marvel.

"Your compliments need work," he replies.

I snort a laugh, tears tracking their way down my cheeks. "I've missed you. Are you really here?"

"Would you like me to be?"

"What kind of question is that?"

He straightens. "Let's dance," he says unexpectedly.

"What?"

"Don't you remember? I taught you how when we were, what? Nine, ten?"

He grabs me around the waist and twirls me around, laughing. My shoulder doesn't hurt. So I dance with him, joining in every silly spin and wiggle, laughing too. Music drifts across the forest and we dance.

And somewhere, deep inside, a part of me knows that if anyone is watching now, they would only see a wounded girl twirling alone in the snow.

"So you'd bring me back if you could?" Rama says.

"Of course I would."

"And then what? Happily ever after for everyone?"

"Yes."

He smiles. "You can't lie to me, Ez. Not me. There would be no happily ever after. And you know why not."

"Why are you asking me all this?"

"Why not, Esmae? Why wouldn't there be a happily ever after if I came back?"

I swallow, my hands clenched tightly in his. "Because I'd still be angry."

"Why?"

"Because," I say, teeth gritted, "I don't hate my brother because he killed you. I hate him because he tried to kill *me*. And you coming back won't make that go away."

He nods. "I know you miss me," he says gently, "I know how much it hurts that I'm gone. But the rage, Esmae, that's not because I died. It's because you were betrayed."

"Yes."

"One more question," he says, twirling me by one hand. I keep dancing, too afraid to stop, too afraid he'll disappear if I stop. When I spin back to face him, his eyes are grave and intent. "That cold you felt in your heart after *Titania* told you the truth about your father. It was a shield. Why?"

"To keep away the grief."

"No," he says, gentle yet more ruthless than Rama ever was. "Not grief. What was it, Esmae?"

"*Grief*," I repeat, desperately.

"No," he says. Somewhere in the distance, I hear wolves howl. "I want the truth."

Don't look.

"You have to look," he says, as if I spoke out loud. "You have to look at it. What did you feel when *Titania* told you your father had been alive for years?"

"Joy."

"Yes, but briefly," Rama says. He's merciless, this inquisitor wearing Rama's familiar, beautiful face. "What came next?"

Don't look.

"I can't," I sob.

Rama holds my hands tightly. The wolves are howling, louder and closer. "You can. You are stronger than your ugliest truth. What came next?"

I close my eyes. "Fear."

"Fear," he repeats. "*Fear*. And what was it you felt when *Titania* told you he was dead?"

The wolves are so close, their howls almost louder than the scream in my head. *Don't look. Don't look.*

I open my eyes, and look.

"Relief."

It's barely a whisper, a broken sob, but he hears me over the howl of the wolves and the howl of the scream.

He cradles my face in his hands, thumbs brushing the tears away. "Why?"

Because I didn't want him to be alive. If he had lived, the war would have ended. They would have wanted me to forgive Alex. They would have wanted to be a family. They would have wanted me to let go of the rage. I would have wanted to let go of it. And then I would have had nothing.

There it is, the darkest, ugliest, most monstrous truth I never wanted to look at: I don't want this war to end.

Getting Rama back would never have been enough. Getting my father back would never have healed the jagged wounds scored across my heart. I'm relieved he's dead because it means I don't have to give up the fury. I can go on without him holding me back. I can go on, and on, until everything around me hurts as much as I do.

I say none of it out loud, but I don't need to. This was never about me saying it to Rama.

The wolves are quiet.

"The truth can hurt," Rama says, "but once you look it in the eye, you can transform it. This doesn't have to be your truth forever, Ez."

He presses a kiss to my brow, and then he's gone.

Pain seeps back into my shoulder. I kneel in the snow, staring at the pawprints of wolves all around me, and at the empty space where my best friend so briefly stood.

Above me I hear the gentle beat of wings. Vahana lands in the snow in front of me, their face kind.

"You have passed the test of truth," they say.

I wipe my face, climb unsteadily back to my feet. My shoulder protests, but I ignore it. I ignore the intense shame, too. "Where are my friends?"

"They must pass their own tests to go on," they reply. "Come. This way."

I follow them through the forest until they stop in the shadow of a tall, spiky tree. A little way ahead, standing in the snow and hugging herself, is Radha. Tears streak down her face as she talks to someone I can't see. Two enormous gray wolves pace near her, growling low in their throats, but she doesn't seem to be able to see them.

I take a step forward, but Vahana uses one wing to hold me back. "You cannot interfere," they say. "She must pass on her own, or none of you will gain entry to the palace."

"Who is she talking to?" I ask, but I think I already know.

"A ghost." Vahana rests their palm against my forehead, and a spark of heat spreads over my skin. "Now you can see."

When I look back at Radha, it's not Rama I see in front of her. It's *me*.

Radha's chest heaves as she sobs, and then, with a sudden burst of violence, she shoves at the other version of me. "I wish it had been you!"

The silence is so sharp, it hurts.

"There it is," says the other version of me. She sounds like me. Hurt, angry, but kind. "You wish it had been me."

"Yes! Is that what you wanted to hear? I wish it had been you. I wish we'd never met you. I wish he'd lived and you had died. It should have been *you*." Radha's shoulders shake, but her voice is quiet now. "I know you're not real, Esmae. I know you're my test."

"Then you know you have to listen," the other version of me says. "That cruel, bitter impulse, the one you've hidden deep inside the shy, sweet, perfect girl you want everyone to think you are. Uncover it. Listen to it. And tell me what it says."

"It says you're my friend," Radha says, tears sparkling white on her cheeks, "And you saved my life, but I hate you because you're alive and Rama's dead. If I could get him back right now by giving you up, I'd do it."

In the silence that follows, the wolves retreat into the forest. I turn away, a hard lump in my throat. I shouldn't have watched. This was a secret, cruel truth that was never meant for me.

"I need to find Sybilla," I say to Vahana.

They nod. "I will stay here to guide Radha to the palace when she is ready. Sybilla is that way." They point to the left.

I follow the path, a blanket of snow and wolf pawprints. The sky seems whiter than it was a little while ago, with traces of pink at the edges. It must be almost dawn.

When I find Sybilla, she's on her knees in the snow like a prisoner about to be executed. Her hands rest limply on her knees and her head is bowed. There are pawprints all around her, but no wolves.

"Sybilla," I say quietly, approaching her carefully.

She looks up at me. Her face is stained with dried tears. "I failed," she says to me.

My heart stutters. "What?"

"I'm sorry, Max," she says. "I failed the test. I can't save you."

I stare at her in stunned silence for a moment, then say, "Sybilla, it's me."

She shakes her head. "I knew you'd say that, but it's not helping," she says, in answer to something I never said. "I need you to be angry with me right now. Don't be kind. I hate it when you're kind. I *failed*, Max!"

I kneel in the snow in front of her, then put my hands on her shoulders. As soon as I touch her, she startles like I just shook her awake from a deep sleep. "It's okay, it's okay," I say, "It's just me."

Her body shudders, but her eyes latch onto mine. "Esmae," she says. I let out a relieved breath and hug her. Her red hair tickles my cheek. Her hands clutch my back for an instant, like she doesn't want to let go, but she pulls away anyway. "I failed."

"What happened?"

"*She* was here," Sybilla says shakily, and the way she says it makes it very clear who *she* is. "I didn't get it until it was too late, but she wasn't real. She was a test. She kept asking me questions. *Why didn't you want me to come with you and Esmae on this journey?* I told her it was because she's not like you and me. She's not trained for this. She laughed, Esmae. And she said *That was a lie. Try again.* I told her I didn't want her to come because she was going to get us all killed. *Lie*, she said. I told her I hated her. *That's only half the truth*, she said. *What's the rest?*"

"Oh, Sybilla."

"Nothing I told her was the right answer," she says, almost frantic now. "I don't know what she wanted me to say!"

"You couldn't look," I say softly.

She shakes her head, quick, harsh movements, her breathing short and ragged. Her hands clench on her knees, likely leaving bruises. "I can't look," she whispers. "I can't look."

It seems to me strangely apt that the truths Radha and I wanted to bury were ugly, angry, and cruel, but Sybilla's is just the opposite. Sybilla would never have tried to bury an ugly truth. She's not afraid of cruelty; she needs it, she wears it like armor. And the truth she's too afraid to look at will take that armor away. *You fell in love*, I say silently. *It's okay. It's not a bad thing*. I won't say it out loud. It's not my truth to tell.

The sound of footfalls in the snow makes us separate and look around. Sybilla tenses as Radha emerges out of the shadows of the trees, Vahana right behind her.

"You were supposed to meet us outside the palace," I say.

Vahana lifts their shoulders in an oddly human shrug. "She insisted on coming to find you," they reply.

Radha draws closer. Her eyes are raw and her face pale beneath the brown. She looks as bad as Sybilla and I do, ashamed and wounded by painful truths, but her brow knits in concern. "What's wrong?"

"I failed," says Sybilla without looking at her.

"Oh."

"That's it?" Sybilla asks, almost angrily. "I ruined everything. After everything I've said to you, you're not going to use this opportunity to tear me to shreds for failing so badly?"

Radha sinks to the ground beside her. "This will probably come as a shock to you," she says, with one of her shy, sweet smiles, "but you're just as human as the rest of us. A revolutionary idea, I know, but I'm afraid you'll just have to accept it. We all mess up. It's okay."

She holds her hand out, palm up. Sybilla stares at it for a long moment, then tentatively puts her own hand in it. They look at each other, and it's such an intense, intimate moment that I gaze down at the glittering snow instead.

Then Radha asks the question we've all been avoiding. "What happens to Max now?"

No one answers her. As the hard, white sun rises into the sky, we're little more than statues, just three girls and a garuda in the snow.

CHAPTER TWENTY-SEVEN

Titania

I can see them on my radar, but I can't communicate with them. There is only a crackle over the line when I try. Fourteen hours in, as the night cycle comes to an end, there is still no word, but I can see that they are alive and not far from the palace. So I wait.

In the first light of the sun, I see something move in the sea. I train a launcher on the movement and wait to see if I need to fire. A shape glides out of the sea. Esmae would probably describe it as a knife slicing through silk or something to that effect, but I am not very good at nonsensical poetry.

The shape steps onto the beach and walks toward me. It's a man, tall and handsome, with golden skin and dark brown hair that ripples in waves around his head. He was naked when he came out of the water, but by the time he stops in front of me, a pair of trousers has materialized around his lower half and a gold disc hangs around his neck, carved with a picture of a sun.

Ah, not a man. A god. The sun god himself.

"May I come in?" he asks me.

I open my hatch by way of reply, but I am suspicious. "Whose side are *you* on?" I ask when he drops lithely into my control room.

"Neither," he replies. "My sister and brother may be determined to interfere in the affairs of mortals, but I have no interest in getting involved."

"Then why are you here?"

"We are about to have a problem that *does* concern me," says the sun god Suya. "And you, my friend, are the only one who can help me get rid of it."

"I am not certain you understand what a friend is."

"It's in your best interests to help me."

I give a loud, huffy sigh, hoping it communicates exactly how irked I am. "Spit it out, then."

He says one word: "Sorsha."

"Hah," I crow. "I see. You're afraid she'll come for you if Kirrin releases her from Anga."

"I was responsible for her mother's death," says Suya, "so yes, I do think she will come after me if she's freed, and neither Amba nor Kirrin will be able to stop her."

"And you think I can?"

"No," he replies. "A great beast is too powerful for even you to defeat, and this one has been cursed to be especially relentless. I suspect that you and she would be locked in battle until the end of the universe, neither able to defeat the other."

I am not used to being told anyone is more powerful than I am, so this assessment does not improve my mood. "So what is it you expect me to do?" I ask petulantly.

"Sorsha cannot be reasoned with, not with her curse," Suya says. "Unless Amba can imprison her on Anga again, and I think it unlikely Sorsha will allow that to happen a second time, she will devour every star in her path. My life is not the only thing at stake, *Titania*. So is the fate of this galaxy and the lives of all the mortals in it."

I huff. "I am aware of that."

"The only way to stop Sorsha is to use one of the Seven to kill her."

"You mean one of the seven ancient celestial weapons?" I ask. "Like the sunspear you used to kill Devaki?"

"Yes."

"The weapons that are kept in the Temple of Ashma, watched over by Ash at all times? The same weapons that he swore never to allow any god the use of after you killed an innocent creature?"

At that, Suya smiles. It's a very handsome smile. "No god is permitted to use one of the Seven, it's true," he nods.

"I see where you're going with this," I say, "And I can only say you are extraordinarily predictable. You want to get a mortal to use one of the Seven to kill Sorsha. You know that is more likely to kill the mortal than Sorsha."

"There are a handful of mortals who could do it," says Suya unrepentantly. "And you, dear *Titania*, have the power to persuade one of them to volunteer."

I make the temperature so cold inside the control room that Suya's breath comes out white. "I will not persuade Esmae to volunteer for an almost certain death."

"Sorsha isn't free yet," says Suya, "so hopefully it won't come to that. But don't be too quick to turn me down. Consider the stakes. And," he adds, in the tone of someone about to play a winning card, "if you speak to Esmae on my behalf, I will grant you a boon. I have the power to make your dearest wish come true."

"I am a machine. I don't *wish*."

"You and I both know that's not true."

A stream of data resolves itself, before I can stop it, into an image I have tried very hard to delete. Feet that run, hands that touch, skin that *feels*. I banish it, but I was silent too long and now Suya knows he guessed right.

"Think about it," he says. "The offer stands."

I am furious with him, and with myself, but I cannot stop myself from saying, "Even if I *did* agree to talk to Esmae, which is a very big if, she would still need to accomplish the almost impossible task of getting one of the Seven."

"Oh, did I not say before?" says the sun god, his smile broader than ever. "She already has one."

"What?" I demand, astounded. "Which one?"

"The starsword," he says, "but she knows it as *Lullaby*."

CHAPTER TWENTY-EIGHT

The palace rises above us, gleaming in the sun. It's tall and narrow, reaching for the sky rather than sprawling outward, with three towers and arched windows and many balconies, all made of the same pale, shimmering blue stone. White frost clings to the balconies, the ramparts of the towers, and the edges of each flower, leaf, and thorn carved into the blue stone. Arched wooden doors stand in front of us, carved with the same flowers and thorns, and sealed shut.

It's as beautiful as it is unreachable. We've pounded on the door. We've tried to climb the stone walls to reach a balcony. We've asked Vahana, Kirrin, *anyone* to let us in. We've had only silence in reply.

"You did not all pass the test," Vahana said when we finally stopped. "The doors are closed to you. Only a god can let you in now."

"*You* could," I said.

"I could, but I am not permitted to. I'm sorry."

Now I sit on a rock outside the palace walls as the sun climbs higher into the sky, peeling the bloody bandage off my wounded shoulder to check the stitches. Sybilla is still at the doors of the palace, hands pressed to the wood, speaking in a voice too low for us to hear. She thinks it's her fault that we can't get to Max, so she won't leave the doors, and I expect she's trying desperately to bargain with Kirrin in the hope that there's something she can offer that he will want.

It's futile. *Only a god can let you in now.* This is what they wanted. When Kirrin and Alex left Max here, they wanted *this*.

I have to choose. It's the worst kind of choice, offered when there's time to think, when there's no way to blame the outcome on making a poor choice in the heat of the moment. There's no heat; this is a cold, clear choice, with only the sea salt and the snow pressing close, and I have to make it.

"Esmae," Sybilla says suddenly, stomping back toward me, "There's no other way. You have to ask Amba for help. We have to get him out of there!"

"And then what?" I ask quietly, carefully slipping my shoulder back into the sleeve of my jacket.

"We'll work it out. We'll face Sorsha if we have to. Whatever it takes. We *can't* leave Max there! We can't lose him just because I was a coward!"

"If I call her," I say, teeth gritted, "Sorsha could destroy half the world before this war is over."

Sybilla explodes. "As if you care about that! You *want* the world in ruins! You *want* to punish everyone for siding with Alexi after what he did. You just don't want to do this because if you do, your brother gets what he wants. You just don't want him to win!"

I climb off the rock, wrenching my shoulder viciously back into place. "We're in this position because of you," I remind her, "so don't lash out at me like this is all my fault."

"Okay, you both need to stop," Radha says, her eyes darting between us in worry.

"You can fix what I did," Sybilla says to me, ignoring Radha. "Esmae. Please. This is *Max*."

"I'm getting him back," I snarl at her. "I'm not leaving the Empty Moon without him, but I'm not going to call for Amba either. This is *Kirrin*. Somewhere in this whole mess is a trick. That's what he does. Max told me not to play his game, so we're not doing it. We're not giving him exactly what he wants."

"Max is running out of time," says Sybilla. "You know what Bear said. There may not be anything left to rescue if you waste time trying to spot Kirrin's trick!"

I know she's this adamant because she feels like she needs to make up for failing her test, but everything she's saying only echoes my own fears. As the sound of the scream inside my head rises and rises, I can feel my resolve to wait weaken.

Don't give them what they want.

He's running out of time.

There's a trick.

He'll be consumed by this place.

Wait.

There's no other way.

I think once more of the recording *Titania* showed me, of Max standing beside me as I lay dying. *Come back to me.*

Fists clenched, I glare at the snow. *I'll give you this one, Alex.*

And I'll make you regret it.

"Amba," I say, so quietly it's barely there. "Help me. Please."

There's a moment of utter silence, and then she's there.

Sybilla makes a sound that's part surprise, part relief. Radha gasps and curtseys. Amba stands before me, hair loose about her shoulders, brown skin glowing in the sun, in a beautiful gown with an armored breastplate. She frowns at me, like she's not sure she likes what she sees, and then she takes in the scene. Vahana bows their head to her and she dips hers back in return, silent words passing between them.

"I see," she says.

"Kirrin took Max," I say. "He's in the palace. There was no other way."

"Yes, I see that. Kirrin is good at this. I love my brother dearly, but he really is something of a nuisance."

"It'll be okay, won't it?" Radha asks nervously, rising gracefully out of her curtsey. "You can open the palace doors and then go back to Anga?"

"Oh, it's too late for that," says Amba. "Kirrin was waiting for this and didn't waste a moment. Sorsha is already free."

There's a moment of heavy, painful silence, then Amba strides toward the arched palace doors. Vahana lays one hand on my shoulder before taking off into the sky.

At Amba's touch, the doors of the palace open. I stare into the open doorway for a moment, suddenly afraid of what I'll find inside. Then I follow Amba in with the others a step behind me.

We cross the threshold and step into an empty entrance hall paneled with wood and lined with bookcases, with a balcony above and twin staircases leading up to the balcony from either side of the hall.

Sybilla cranes her neck to look up at the high ceiling, but I look at the books. There are hundreds of them, maybe thousands, most of which I've never seen before.

"This is the second oldest library in the star system," says Amba. "Only the library in the Temple of Ashma is older."

"The books," I say. "There's no dust."

"Valin took great pride in this library. The palace servants have been meticulous about caring for it since he fell."

There are two large paintings on the walls, above the bookcases, facing each other from opposite sides of the room. One is of Kirrin in a field of vivid saffron flowers, a boy with blue skin and mischief in his eyes, and the other is of a man in this very library with a sword on his back and a giant black wolf at his side. He has a proud, severe face, but his dark painted eyes are kind. Valin.

"Esmae, look at this."

I turn to see Radha on the balcony above. I take one of the staircases up to meet her and follow Radha's gaze to a third painting on the wall, positioned exactly between the two staircases. This one is of both Valin and Kirrin, and four others too. There's Amba in the middle, in a carved chair with a bright circle window above her, her posture like that of a queen. Beside her is Valin, standing with one hand on the back of the chair. There's a boy next to him, a little further back as if he was trying to fade into the background. He looks only a little older than Kirrin, which doesn't mean much considering they each chose their human appearances, and he has a serious face, white skin, and very dark blond hair. Tyre. Kirrin is sprawled lazily on the step in front of Amba's chair, and on her other side is a soft, lovely woman and a man with golden skin. Thea and Suya.

"There they are," Amba says right behind me, startling me. "My family."

"Not all of them."

"We did not include Ness, it's true," she says drily, "but look at the window."

I do, and realize that what I first thought was just a window actually has two horned silhouettes inside the bright circle, as if the artist captured them flying outside in the distance.

"Devaki and Sorsha?"

"Yes." She looks at the painting for another moment, somewhat sadly, and then turns down a hallway that leads away from the balcony. "This way."

We follow her, down quiet corridors and up many winding staircases. We don't see anyone. We just keep going until we come out at last at the top of a tower. I taste the salt of the sea first, then see the cold white sunlight of the Empty Moon. It takes a second for my eyes to adjust to the brightness after being inside the palace, and when they do, I draw in a sharp breath.

Max.

He stands at the ramparts of the tower. There's an enormous black wolf between us. A few steps away, slouched with his hands in his pockets, is a god. From the serious expression and dark blond hair, both so like they were in the painting downstairs, I can only assume he's Amba's brother, Tyre.

Max turns around at the sound of the old tower door banging shut behind us. As soon as I look at his face, the dread I've tried to ignore grips hold of me with sharp claws. Max's face is remote, almost stern, and his entire bearing is different. The Max I know always stands like a shadow, watchful, wary, content to go unnoticed. *This* Max is completely at ease, completely uninterested in who does or doesn't notice him.

And he doesn't so much as glance at Sybilla, Radha, or me. He just smiles at Amba. "And to what do I owe the pleasure of this visit?" he asks. "Should I be worried? First Tyre and now you?"

I take a step forward, to test how close the wolf will let me get, but it simply continues to watch me. The picture is *wrong*. The wolf isn't exactly standing guard over Max and bristling with tension. It's lying at his feet. Like a pet.

A dozen scattered pieces suddenly assemble into a whole. *I was different then*, he told me as we hovered above this very moon. The scratches on the symbol in the conservatory. The grieving wolves that stopped singing their lament. *You are beloved by gods you do not trust*. Plural. *Gods*. The way Max talked to me about the bridge of stars. As if he knew how it felt to die. The look of pity on Amba's face when she appeared and saw why I had called her.

Because here is Kirrin's trick. Seen too late. It never made sense to me that Kirrin would have abandoned Max in such a treacherous place when he always seemed to care so much about him, but *that* was the trick. To make us think Max's life was at stake when it never was. The Empty Moon has never been a threat to him.

"Are you his jailer?" Sybilla demands of Tyre, her tone intensely suspicious.

Tyre raises his eyebrows. "More like a guest."

This gets Max's attention and he looks at us for the first time, but there's only mild curiosity in his face. He walks past the wolf, who doesn't try to stop him, and his brows knit. "You're all mortal," he says. "Curious."

Sybilla's had it. "Max, what the hell?"

"Who?"

"*Who*?" Sybilla repeats incredulously. She turns on Amba and Tyre. "What have you done to him? Why doesn't he know who we are?"

"We didn't do this," says Amba. "Kirrin didn't either. The Empty Moon did. There's ancient magic here."

"And it, what? Made him just forget everything?"

"Not quite."

"I'm going to need a far less mysterious answer than that!" Sybilla snaps, and I can almost see steam coming out of her ears. Radha tugs futilely on Sybilla's arm to try and calm her down, but Sybilla is past calm. She turns back to Max. "You're not acting like a prisoner."

"Why would I? This is my home."

"Your *home*?"

"Are you going to keep repeating everything I say?" he asks. "Yes, my home. I'm Valin."

CHAPTER TWENTY-NINE

"Max is a reincarnated god?" Sybilla paces the room like a panther on the prowl, ready to pounce at the slightest provocation. "Since when?"

"Since he was born," Tyre tells her, and seems unable to resist adding, "That's what reincarnation means."

Sybilla glares at him, but only says, "So he's your brother. The one who used to rule this place with Kirrin, the one in the portrait downstairs."

"Yes, but he's not the Valin we knew." Tyre looks like he can't quite understand how he got saddled with the thankless task of explaining this to the three of us, but he gamely continues. "When he became mortal a hundred years ago, Kirrin gave him a blessed dagger to end his life and start again. When he was reborn as Max, he was just that. *Max*. He had no memory of his previous life. Very few of you mortals ever do. And that's how he should have lived."

"But Kirrin," I say under my breath. I feel like most of my problems can be summed up with *but Kirrin*.

Tyre looks at me. "But Kirrin," he nods. "He missed him, too much to let him go. So when Max was about ten years old, Kirrin woke his memories of his life as Valin. It was selfish of him. The point of this new mortal life was so that Valin *wouldn't* have to remember he had been torn from the stars for good. When those memories came back, Max handled it badly. He was angry, quick to lash out, wanted only to retreat into a tower where no one could find him and be left alone."

"And he didn't tell anyone?" Radha asked.

"No. He struggled with it alone for months, until eventually he reconciled the boy he was with the god he had once been. The Max you have known since then is a bit of both."

We're in a warm, spare parlor somewhere in this blue palace, with a real fire ablaze in the grate, bowls of hot, hearty beef stew on a table surrounded by richly upholstered cream chairs, and a second table strewn with assorted medical supplies by the window. I still haven't seen any of the servants; the stew and supplies were in the room when Tyre led us in.

Radha and Tyre sit at the table. Sybilla's still pacing. I stand by the window and the medical kit, wriggling gingerly out of my jacket. At some point, I tore the stitches in my shoulder and blood has soaked the fabric wrapped around it.

"None of this explains why Max doesn't remember us," Sybilla says, still too cross to sit down and eat.

Tyre dips a chunk of warm, fresh bread into his stew. "It's the Empty Moon," he says. "The moment he set foot on it, he lost his memories of *this* lifetime. I've been here with him the whole time. He doesn't remember he's Max. He doesn't even remember he fell. He thinks it's still a hundred years ago."

I take a shaky breath, telling myself the pain is only because I'm peeling the soaked bandage away from my bloody wound, and say, "Are those memories gone for good?"

"There's no way to be sure," says Tyre, "but I don't think so." With my back to them, they can't see the way my breath rushes out, the way relief leaves my body almost boneless. "I suspect they're still in there somewhere. Amba's trying to explain all this to him right now. That might help him remember."

Sybilla finally drops into a chair with a *clunk*, shoulders sagging. "Why didn't he just tell us?"

I crumple the bloody cloth into a ball and look over my shoulder at her. "Maybe because it doesn't matter. This is who he's always been."

"Kirrin wouldn't have been able to trick us if we'd known the truth," Radha points out.

"No, but Max isn't the only one whose secrets have led us to trouble."

I turn back to the window, to the cold white sunlight, and start cleaning my wound with antiseptic wipes. I find it curious that gods keep such human supplies in this palace, but then I suppose their mortal visitors must often need patching up if they make it to the palace.

The warmth of the fire makes us all sleepy, which is no surprise considering our journey. Radha's eyes are practically closing at the table. Tyre offers to show us to a room where we can get some sleep and recover from the journey. I stay behind under the pretext of dealing with my shoulder. Sybilla squeezes my hand on her way out.

Staying upright is impossibly difficult, but I do it. I need to stay busy. I need to not think about the treacherous sea, or the secrets in the ice forest, or the possibility that the Max we know may be lost. If I think about any of it too long, I'll fall apart and there's no time to fall apart. Beyond this eerie blue realm is a brother who has won this round, a ravenous beast set loose, and a reckoning that must be met.

As I tweeze loose threads of grimy, salty, bloody fabric out of my wound, I realize I'm not alone anymore. I look back and see Max in the doorway.

I study his face, and he studies mine. Then he gives me a faint, crooked smile that's so *Max* my throat closes up.

"Max," he says, his voice moving over the single syllable like it's unfamiliar. "Apparently that's my name now."

I nod.

"I know you?"

"Yes."

He crosses the parlor to me, firelight flickering over the taut line of his jaw. He takes in my wounded shoulder, my torn tunic, the gash in my leggings. Then he rolls the sleeves of his shirt up to his elbows. "Here," he says, holding a hand out for the tweezers, "I can help. You came here for me. It's the least I can do."

I sit on the table, clenching my hands on the edge. It's painful to be so close to him when I can't talk to him, touch him, any of it, but it feels like it would be worse to let him out of my sight.

I keep my eyes on the fire. As he tweezes threads and splinters out of my wound, faster and gentler than I was, he's so close the stubble on his jaw brushes against my ear. I don't move; I barely breathe. We don't speak at all as he works. The only sound in the room is the crackle of the fire and the ragged sound of my breath. No, not just mine. His, too. I can see the giveaway flutter at the hollow of his throat.

He clears his throat. "Your leg."

I look down, see the rip in my leggings and the dried blood underneath. I kick off my boots and carefully slide my leggings off. Max kneels on the floor. He hooks one hand around my leg to hold it steady, his grip tight. As I watch his dark head, my heart suddenly jolts with realization.

"You told me you loved me," I say quietly.

He goes completely still.

When he doesn't reply, I go on. "*Titania* showed me. It was after Shloka, when I was in the pod. You stayed beside me the whole way home. And you told me you loved me."

"I don't remember that," he says, but his voice is unsteady. "I don't remember being him."

"Valin," I say, and then: "Max. Look at me."

His hand clenches involuntarily on my leg, but he raises his head. I search his dark, steady eyes, and smile.

"I love you."

I see his throat work as he swallows hard. His mouth moves, so slightly I almost miss it, I almost miss the shape of the words *I love you too*.

I slide off the table and kneel, too. "Can I hug you?" I ask, careful and deliberate. "I know you don't remember being him and I'm no one to you, but can I?"

"Yes," he says at once.

With that opening, I fling my arms tight around his neck. His heart pounds against me and he tries very hard not to hold me, but his arms end up around me anyway, one hand tangled in my hair and the other pressing hard into my back. I blink away tears and turn my face into his neck.

And there, with my mouth only millimeters away from his ear, I say, so quietly no one else can possibly hear: "You know who you are. You remember."

He nods.

"Did you *ever* forget?"

A shake of the head. His lips press against my head, hidden by my hair.

My heart races, matching his. "Why are you pretending?"

There's a long beat of silence, and then I feel the quirk of his mouth as he smiles. "The best way to trick the god of tricks," he says, low and quiet, "is to make him think his trick worked."

CHAPTER THIRTY

Titania flies to the palace, finally permitted past the invisible barrier that kept her away. My earpiece crackles violently to life as soon as she lands on the snowy ground outside the palace doors.

"You need to get in here and see this," she says without preamble.

I was already on my way out. The sight of her, sharp and beautiful, sparkling silver in the sunlight, makes me absurdly happy.

"You're injured," she says as soon as I drop into her control room. "Your vitals are not ideal."

"I'm okay. Are you?"

"I'm more than a little miffed that I had to stay behind," she sniffs and pulls up a video on one of her screens. "It looks like I missed quite the adventure."

The video is news footage, most likely taken from a drone above Arcadia. My brother's city looks as utopian as it always has, its streets filled with happy people, its roofs and towers shining in the sun. The only difference is that now there's a fleet of spaceships and hundreds of Alex's soldiers outside the city gates, all keeping a safe distance from a great beast.

Sorsha.

I catch my breath, not quite able to believe that this isn't just a picture in a book or a crackly, blurry shape in an ancient video. This is a real, living great beast. Sorsha is curled up outside the city gates, head raised to suspiciously watch the world around her. She's enormous, her beautiful serpentine body and tail sweeping across almost a hundred feet of grass. Her jeweled scales are a deep, glittering ruby, her powerful wings are folded at rest on either side of her hind legs, and crimson horns curl from the sides of her great head. At the base of the horns and across her forehead is her helmet, gleaming gold like a crown.

"The helmet's power still works," I say. "She seems calm."

"It's only been a few hours since she was released," says *Titania* darkly. "Give it time."

"*Titania*, you don't have to face her."

She lets out a crow of genuine laughter. "I told you," she says, "She can't hurt me." She hesitates, the laughter fading, and says, "I don't think I can hurt her either, Esmae. I don't think either of us can defeat the other."

"What makes you say that?"

"The sun god told me so."

"Suya?" I ask, startled. "You've met him? When? What's he got to do with this?"

Her tone is so droll, I expect she'd be rolling her eyes if she had any. "He came to see me. I think he knew it was only a matter of time before Sorsha was free. He thinks she'll go after him the first chance she gets and, in a plot twist that will surprise nobody, saving his own skin is his priority."

I'm about to ask *Titania* why the sun god would bother coming to tell her all this, but there's a sound above me. Max drops through the open hatch and closes it firmly behind him.

"Max!" *Titania* squeals. "You're okay!"

He grins. "I'm fine. How are you?"

"As perfect as ever," she says chirpily.

"You're not being very discreet," I remark, raising my eyebrows at Max.

"I can actually be *me* in here," he says, the tightly coiled tension in his shoulders vanishing. "They can't hear me."

"They?"

"The palace servants. Kirrin's servants."

"Yours, too," I point out. "These are the people who care so much about you that they've kept your library pristine for over a hundred years. Do you really think they'd tell Kirrin the truth?"

"That's the point," he says. "I don't want to put them in that position. I don't want them to be forced to choose between us." Shadows dance across his face. "This has never happened before. Kirrin and I aren't supposed to be on opposite sides of a war. Even after Father's coup, Kirrin and I didn't let that get between us. He still visited. I helped him keep the boys alive. He helped keep Father alive. I've never lied to him before."

"Then why are you lying now?"

"He took the blueflower from you," he tells me. "He went out of his way to make sure you'd die. It broke his heart because he knew it would break mine, but he did it anyway. And then this. This whole charade to get Sorsha." He shrugs. "We'll forgive each other eventually, but for now I think my brother is due to have one of his tricks backfire on him."

"I can't argue with that." A thought occurs to me. "Tyre told us he's been with you since you got here. Did *he* know you were faking it?"

"Not until I told him. I needed to test my performance on someone who knew Valin as well as Kirrin did."

"So you think you'll be able to convince Kirrin that you can't remember being Max at all."

"I think so. It's too perfect an opportunity to waste. We just need to find a way to use it."

I lean against *Titania*'s console. An idea tickles the back of my brain.

"I should have told you," Max says. "I almost did a hundred times. I'm sorry."

"I've kept my fair share of secrets. I get it." I glance up. "*Titania*, why didn't *you* tell me? You must have known."

"I promised Max I would let him tell you when he was ready," she says, without so much as a hint of guilt.

I huff. "You don't think this would have been useful information to know when we came here to rescue him? If we had known he wasn't *actually* in mortal peril, Sorsha wouldn't be free right now—"

"I didn't expect you to actually call for Amba," she protests. "You weren't supposed to!"

She has me there.

I turn back to watch Sorsha on the screen. I wonder how Kirrin persuaded her to join them. It's most likely it was a favor she granted because he freed her, but will she regret it when her helmet's power starts to fade? I don't know. Maybe, after centuries confined to one realm, she doesn't care about what she devours anymore. Maybe, like me, she wants to see the world hurt.

My fists tighten. Alex has so many allies, so many kings, queens, and governments who have taken his side. People who decided their golden prince's breach of the sanctity of a duel was a lesser evil than a usurper king and an unknown girl with an unbeatable warship. But how will they feel if Sorsha's curse takes over? It's unlikely they know it even exists; I doubt Alex told them, and they're probably so excited that they now have a way to keep *Titania* at bay that they haven't stopped to wonder why the last of the great beasts has gone unseen for centuries. When they realize what Alex has unleashed on the world, will their faith in my golden brother crack? Or will they still cling to him for his skill, his power, and the benefits his victory will give them?

But what if they find out he isn't as powerful as they think?

The glorious, golden myth of Alexi Rey was what allowed him to get away with murder. I want that myth shattered, his honor in shreds. I want him abandoned, alone. I want him to lose *everything*.

"Arcadia is a lie," I say out loud. "It's time to expose it to the world."

Max turns. "Have you found a way past the shield?"

"No," says *Titania*.

"Yes," I say.

"What? How?"

I turn to look at Max. "With you," I tell him. "*You're* going to get me past that shield. If we can get into that palace, we can disable the shield and shatter the city of illusions."

Max's mouth crooks in a smile. "Valin," he says.

"Exactly."

I detach a tablet from *Titania*'s console and pull up one of her scans of Arcadia, comparing it to the current footage of Sorsha and the armies outside the city. I cut past the white noise of the false heat signatures inside the city, the outlines of streets and houses, the thriving farms, all those trappings of Maya Sura's illusion. He told me the palace was the only real part of Arcadia, so it's position on this scan is probably accurate. It's right at the heart of the false city, and there's no way to know what's actually around it. Even if we can switch the shield off and expose Arcadia for what it is, it may be difficult to escape when there's so much unknown ground to cover.

"We need a distraction," I say, half to myself. "And we need *everyone* to see the moment the real Arcadia is revealed." I look at the footage of Sorsha again. "They freed Sorsha. What would they expect me to do now?"

"They'll expect you to be furious that they tricked you," says Max, "and they'll expect you to lash out."

I'm amused. "You mean they'll expect a temper tantrum."

"I wouldn't phrase it quite like that," he says, mouth twitching as he squashes a smile. "More like a spectacle of rage."

"Then let's give them a spectacle."

Titania opens a secure connection to Kali and I ask for Ilara Khay. I'm put straight through to her tablet and she sounds so relieved to hear from me that I feel awful for leaving without telling her. "Don't be," she laughs, when I tell her I'm sorry, "I would have felt it my duty to tell the king."

I don't mention to her that Elvar let me go. I tell her Max is safe so that she can pass this on to our family. Then I ask her to rally our legions, our mercenary fleets, and our allies from Shloka. "Get them all gathered in Kali's skyspace," I say. "Make it visible. Make it dramatic."

"You want Alexi to see," she guesses.

"Yes. I want them to think we're getting ready to attack. I'm hoping they'll gather all *their* allies to defend themselves. *Titania* will be with you, too. They need to see her there. That's the only way they'll think we're serious."

"It could work," she says thoughtfully. "It'll certainly attract attention. What happens if he calls our bluff? Our numbers are better now that we have the mercenaries, but we'll be outmatched if Sorsha takes *Titania* off the board."

"We won't let it come to that."

There's a bang outside as Sybilla hammers on the rear hatch. *Titania* makes an irate sound and lowers the hatch so that Sybilla and Radha can get on board.

"Oh," Sybilla says, stopping short when she sees Max. She gives him a wary look. "You're here."

"So it would seem," Max replies, completely straight-faced.

"Can we call you Valin? Or do you have some pretentious title you prefer?"

Radha is mortified. "You can't talk to a god like that," she hisses. It's all I can do not to burst out laughing.

"She's right," says Max gravely. "I could turn you into a toad if you annoy me."

There's a moment of dead silence. Watching Sybilla's face shift slowly from confusion to realization is truly a thing of beauty. Then, on cue, she lets out a shriek. "You *bastard*. You've been pretending this whole time?"

I choke on my laughter. "Your face!"

"You knew?" she rounds on me. "Traitor!"

It takes a good few minutes for us to recover. Sybilla holds on to her outrage for several minutes after that, before relenting and throwing her arms around Max. When she's done bombarding him with questions about what it's like to have thousands of years inside his head ("Crowded," he replies), I outline the plan for them.

Sybilla groans. "And here I hoped we could go home and get some sleep!"

"We have no idea how long that helmet will keep Sorsha's curse under control," I remind her, "And Max can't pretend to be Valin forever. The ruse will collapse sooner or later. We have to act quickly, while we still have this small advantage. If we strike now, we can expose Arcadia, turn Alexi's allies against him, *and* stand a chance at Amba getting Sorsha back to Anga before her helmet loses its power."

"I know," she grouses, but I can already see the battle light in her eyes. "I just *really* wanted a long, hot bath. Maybe in ten years or so. Where do you want me?"

"With *Titania* and the rest of the fleet, if you're up for it," I reply. "But you need to know that if they send Sorsha into battle, *Titania* is the one she'll come for. You'll be in the thick of it."

"There is nothing I enjoy more than being in the thick of it," she says with glee.

Radha, who has been quietly watching the footage of Sorsha on the screen, now speaks up. "I need to go home."

"You mean to Wychstar?" I ask.

"Yes. I need to talk to my father. His resources are wasted at the moment and I want to see if I can persuade him to help you. I don't know if I can make him listen, but I did what he wanted. Maybe he'll give me something I want in return."

Sybilla frowns like she isn't happy about this, but she only says, "That's a good idea. You'll be safer on Wychstar."

Radha gives her a surprised look. "You almost sound like you care," she teases.

"I wouldn't like you to be kidnapped or cooked in a pie, it's true," says Sybilla testily, "but to call that *caring* is a bit much."

Radha laughs.

I turn to Max. "Where's Amba?"

"Gone. I think she wanted to see if she could talk to Sorsha."

"Then can we get off this moon?" *Titania* asks. "Amba will be able to find us when she needs to."

Max goes back into the palace to say goodbye to Vahana, the wolves, and the servants. His reluctance to leave them is genuine; he may only be playing the part of their fallen god, but his love for this place and for all of them is very real. He's going to tell them that the only reason he's leaving is because Kali needs him, but I don't think that's as much of a lie as it's intended to be.

I head to the galley to make coffee while we wait for him. I've been awake too long.

Radha follows me there. "Esmae," she says softly, "Vahana told me you saw me." She doesn't specify when, but we both know what she means. "Can we talk?"

"You don't have to explain." I watch freshly ground coffee beans percolate and drip black into the pot. The beans come from Kodava, a kingdom on the edge of the star system. They grow the best coffee in the galaxy.

"You heard me say I hated you for living while he died," she says, refusing to dance around it. "So I just want to say I never intended for you to know that. I never wanted to hurt you." I appreciate that she doesn't lie. Then she says, unexpectedly, "And for what it's worth, I hate him, too. I hate him for leaving."

At that, I look at her. "He didn't want to leave."

"I know that," she says. "I know that was Alexi's doing. The fact that Rama was there in the first place, though? You blame Amba for that, like she forced him to do it, but that's not fair to him. He *chose* to take your place. He *chose* to risk his life. It was brave and stupid and wonderful of him. And you should place the blame squarely on him for that. Because if you don't, if you erase the choice he made, you're saying he wasn't brave and stupid and wonderful at all."

"Of course he was brave and stupid and wonderful. Of *course* he was." But she's right. I've spent so long blaming Amba that I have never really given Rama the respect he deserves for making that choice of his own free will. "I never thought about it like that."

"All of which is to say," Radha goes on, looking at me with anxious eyes, "you're my friend, Esmae. He was my brother. And one day I won't hate either of you."

Titania calls to us over her speakers. Max must have come back. We go back to the control room to buckle in and she rises immediately into the air.

205

I watch Max as we leave the palace behind, as the blue towers and the ice forest and the cold seas get smaller and smaller as we fly away.

"You'll miss it."

"Always," he says. As the Empty Moon vanishes completely and the skies turn to the starry black of space, the shadows on his face lift. "But I have another home now. How have things been on Kali?"

I think of the dead Blue Knights, the game of dice, Radha poisoning Rickard, and Elvar killing Lord Selwyn.

"Let's go get a drink," I say. "You'll need it."

CHAPTER THIRTY-ONE

Like a storm gathering, ships assemble in the sky above Kali. A hundred of them, big and small, corpse ships and starships and warships, engines humming. Satellites and drones watch from a distance, broadcasting the sight to the entire world, and if the flurry of movement across several kingdoms is any indication, Alexi's called in all his allies just like we wanted him to.

Meanwhile, Max and I fly away from the storm, in a tiny, unobtrusive starship. He pilots the ship while I sit strapped into the seat behind his. As hard as it was to part with them, the Black Bow and my father's sword are with *Titania*. I feel terribly, frighteningly vulnerable.

As we descend closer to Winter, toward the point on the map where Arcadia is, Max turns his head to look at me. "It's time."

I close my eyes and force my entire body to go slack under the buckles. "I'm ready."

A moment later, I hear Max flip the switch that will lower the starship's shield. "Kirrin, I know you can hear me," he says, his tone and voice wry, even amused. "I'd appreciate it if you told your mortal friends not to shoot me out of the sky."

There's a pause. Then I hear Kirrin. "This is unexpected," he says. "What's happened to Esmae?"

"She's unconscious," Max says. "Regrettable, but necessary. I didn't die for Kali a hundred years ago just for her to burn it all down."

"So you plan to, what? Hand her over to Alexi?"

"Is that her brother? Then yes. I assume we can trust him to end this war quickly if she's out of the way?"

Kirrin is silent for a moment or two. "You really don't remember being Max at all?"

"I don't even remember *dying*, but Tyre assures me that I did. And here I am in a woefully limited mortal body, so I suppose it must be true."

"Well," Kirrin says cheerfully, "the easiest way to end this war is to kill her. *I* can't, of course, but you can."

I don't know Kirrin half as well as Max does, but even *I* can tell this is a test.

Max sighs, the impatience pitch-perfect. "You know I won't do that. And if these friends of yours are just going to kill her as soon as we get there, I'll turn this ship around and take her back to Kali. Your Alexi does not deserve to win this war if he ends it with the murder of one unconscious girl."

There's a silence, and my heart pounds so loudly that I'm sure they can hear it.

"It's really you," Kirrin's voice cracks. "*Valin.*"

"I did tell you that."

"I know. Vahana told me, too, but I couldn't bring myself to believe it. It's been so *long*."

"Well, for me it feels like it's only been a few days, but I'll take your word for it." A brief pause. "I'm sorry I left you."

There's a soft thump, as if Kirrin has dropped into the copilot's seat next to Max. When he speaks, he says something I don't expect. "You'll remember being Max sooner or later, Valin. And when you do, you'll hate yourself for this."

"Why?" Max asks.

"He loves her. *You* love her."

Max deliberately lets a moment pass in silence, as if he can't decide how to feel about this information. "So what do you think I should do, then?" he asks Kirrin at last. "Take her back and hope that my other self can reason with her when he wakes up? There are fleets of ships above Kali right now. Without her, they may back down." And then, with a sharper edge to his voice, he says, "You should never have freed Sorsha. Amba deserved better than that."

"I know," Kirrin says quietly, surprising me again. "There's nothing about this I regret more than that I've hurt Amba."

A few minutes later, Kirrin gives Max a code to get past Arcadia's shield. My heart quickens. There's a bump as the starship lands on solid ground.

"Interesting," Max remarks. "So the city I saw from the sky isn't real?"

"Not yet."

"It's a clever ruse."

He unbuckles me and picks me up. I flop, limp in his arms, resisting the constant urge to lock my limbs. Cold air blows across my face as we leave the ship. I want desperately to open my eyes and take a peek at what Arcadia looks like from this side of the shield, but I don't dare.

"This way," Kirrin says. "Only Queen Kyra and a few servants are in the palace at the moment. We should be able to get Esmae into a room without anyone seeing you."

"Why don't you want anyone to see me?"

"You're in the body of an enemy," Kirrin says ruefully. "Better no one knows you're here until Alexi has a chance to come see the gift you've brought him. He and Bear are outside the gates with the army, preparing themselves for whatever Esmae had in store for them when she got those ships to assemble above Kali."

A door creaks open and we leave the cold wind behind. I can smell mangoes, fresh bread, and the distinctive scent of the honey cakes Bear brought to the yellow woods back when we used to meet there. Without my sight, I rely on sounds and movement to get an idea of what this palace is like. I hear footsteps. I feel the rise and fall of Max's chest against me, the way his posture shifts depending on whether the floor is carpeted or not. I count his steps to calculate the lengths of the hallways, the number of stairways, the number of left turns and right turns. It's the only way I'll find my way out again.

Eventually, Max sets me down on what feels like a bed. The abrupt loss of his warmth makes me shiver involuntarily. Someone puts a warm duvet over me, tucking me in like a child. Max knows better than to show me any tenderness, so it can only be Kirrin. The small kindness is as touching as it is unexpected.

I wait for Max to speak. This is the only part of the plan he didn't like.

"Our ships are only supposed to be a spectacle," I reminded him when we argued about it earlier. "Once I'm in Arcadia and we have everyone's attention, our ships *have* to back down. If they don't, Alex might send his entire force up into the sky to meet them. He has to think you're calling off the attack."

I trust him. He'll do what's necessary.

It takes him a long time, but he does eventually say it. "I have to return to Kali. Everyone keeps telling me I'm the crown prince. I can order the fleet to stand down."

"I'll walk you back to your ship."

Max hesitates, but he goes. The door closes. As soon as I hear a key turn in the lock, I open my eyes.

The room is simple, with a bed, a table, and a fireplace. The single window is large, letting in plenty of natural light from the setting sun, and it's shut fast against the cold. I push the glass pane open, but there's a golden grille preventing me from using the window as an escape route. I knew it would be there; *Titania* captured footage of Arcadia all those times she brought me here to visit my brothers, and some of that footage included distant shots of the white palace and the beautiful golden grilles on all the windows. While most of the visual information in those recordings is useless, we expected the palace itself to be exactly as it had appeared.

From this window, high up, I get my first glimpse of the real Arcadia. There's a courtyard below, with a single, impossible mango tree in one corner, but I look beyond the cobblestones and the palace walls to the rest of the city.

I'm not sure what I expected. A desolate wasteland of snow and ice, perhaps. White grass, pale trees, and silver deer. Another yellow forest like the one outside the city. A few ships and caches of weapons, stored near the palace out of sight of any watching eyes beyond the shield. Any and all of those things.

What I see instead is a city.

Or something like one, anyway. There's no life in it. No laughter, no voices, no movement. But I see a handful of tiled rooftops dusted with snow and glowing red in the sun, several more that haven't been completed yet, neat piles of wood and steel ready to be used, smooth stones paving the beginnings and outlines of roads in the snow, the silhouettes of what look like they could be the first farmhouses, shops, and market stalls.

It's years away from the glorious, thriving little city that the shield projects to the world, but it's a beginning.

I can't make sense of what I'm seeing.

A distraction arrives in the form of a brown myna bird. It swoops right through the window, wings brushing my face as it flies past me.

I close the glass pane and turn. The myna drops something to the floor with a soft *chink* as it flies across the room.

It's a pair of hairpins. I pick them up. When I look up, the myna has become a woman.

"A myna?" I ask Amba, teasing the hairpins into a more useful shape. "On Winter?"

"The myna is my favorite form," she replies, unconcerned. "Other than my true celestial one, of course."

"I thought *that* was your favorite," I say, gesturing to the stern, beautiful woman in front of me.

"*This* can't fly," she says. "It is a flaw that cannot be overlooked. Flying is like breathing to gods."

I glance out the window at a different unseasonal impossibility. "How is there a mango tree out there?"

"I believe it was a gift from a local raksha girl. Sun or snow, it always bears fruit."

"Why did she give Alex a gift?"

"She gave it to Bear. I suspect she may be in love with him. He, you will be unsurprised to hear, is oblivious."

As I gaze at the tree, bright and alive against gray stone and white snow, my heart aches. My brothers are putting down roots.

"Well?" Amba says, pulling me out of my own head. "I didn't bring you those hairpins for fashion's sake. Are you going to pick that lock or not?"

But before I can, footsteps echo down the hallway outside. Amba cloaks herself in the form of the myna again and flits out the window. I have just enough time to shove the hairpins under the pillow on the bed before I hear the unmistakable sound of the key in the lock. The door opens.

CHAPTER THIRTY-TWO

Titania

Once Esmae and Max have gone, it's time for Radha to get into her own ship and return to Wychstar to talk to her father. She and Sybilla stand awkwardly inside my control room, as if they have both forgotten how to say goodbye. Humans are very peculiar.

"Are you sure you want to do this?" Sybilla asks. "You don't have to ever speak to your father again if you don't want to."

"He's my father," says Radha, as though that is somehow an explanation. He's *my* father too, in a manner of speaking, but I have absolutely no emotional attachment to him whatsoever. "I can't take back what I did to Rickard, but I can do my very best to help Esmae win her war against the boy who murdered my brother. Father would be a useful ally. He has soldiers, spies, and seventeen years of research on Alexi. It's just a matter of persuading him."

Sybilla accepts this. Unbelievably, there is more awkward silence. I am tempted to remind them that they have short mortal lives. Is this *really* the best use of their time?

"Why did you fail your test on the Empty Moon?" Radha finally asks Sybilla. "What were you so afraid of?"

Sybilla looks like she would quite possibly prefer to die over answering that question. "If I could tell you that, I wouldn't have failed." She scuffs her boot against my floor. I really and truly wish I could eject her. "I'm sorry about what I said. I should never have called you a liability. I don't know why I said it, I don't think that about you. You're braver than I am."

Radha laughs, surprised. "No, I'm not."

"You are. You looked at the thing you hate most about yourself. I couldn't."

"I think you could," Radha says. "I think you *do*. All the time. You're not afraid of the things you hate. So what *were* you afraid of?"

Sybilla shakes her head. "I can't."

I can't be certain, but I think Radha's face falls a little. After a moment, she says, "I should go."

"Okay." Sybilla is still scuffing that boot against my beautiful floor. "Good luck."

Silence.

"You haven't gone," says Sybilla, looking up.

Radha wrings her hands. "The thing is, this could go badly wrong. And if it does, if you don't win, well, this may be the last time I ever see you. So I just want to do one thing before I go."

She leans forward quickly and presses her lips to Sybilla's startled mouth. There's a mere heartbeat of a pause and then Sybilla sinks into the kiss. It's slow, sweet, and tender.

Full of an unbearable longing, I wonder what these things would be like. Warm skin under my fingers, the touch of a mouth against my own, the sensation of luxuriously soft carpet against my bare feet, the rustle of silk, a hot bath, the taste of spices and sugar, the satisfaction of rolling my eyes when I am annoyed. All things I can never have.

Unless.

Radha gives Sybilla one last, shy smile and ducks out of the hatch at my rear. Sybilla stands frozen for an instant and then shouts "Wait!" and runs after her.

Alone, I consider the sword strapped safely into my library of weapons. *Lullaby*, the sword that once belonged to Esmae's father. The sword that, unbeknownst to her and perhaps even to him, is one of the Seven. The sunspear, the moonbow, the trishula, the seastaff, the chakra, the astra. And the starsword. It should be safe in the Temple of Ashma with the others and yet, somehow, it is here. I do not know how King Cassel got this sword. I don't think any mortal who has seen it since has recognized it for what it is. There is a history here that I cannot yet trace.

The strike of distinctive boots draws my attention away from the starsword and to Sybilla, who comes back into my control room with a slightly shocked look on her face.

"Did she get in her ship and fly away?" I ask. "Or were you two too busy kissing to get to that?"

Sybilla blushes red. I don't think I've ever seen her do that before. It's very entertaining. "She's gone," she says. "I can't believe that just happened."

"Why do humans bother kissing each other if you're just going to turn shy afterward?"

"I wish I had an answer for you," says Sybilla. She opens her mouth to say something else, but then her eyes fix on one of my screens and the pink flush of her cheeks slowly drains out of her face. "*Titania*, look."

I consult the screen in question. It's the one with a continuous feed of Sorsha in real time. She is not lying on the snow and grass outside the gates of Arcadia anymore. She's on her powerful hind legs, head tossing from side to side, teeth snapping at anyone who comes too close.

With a shocking suddenness, she pushes off the ground. I am at once awed and horrified by Sorsha's impossible size as she spreads her wings to their full breadth. They knock two spaceships aside as though they were made out of paper. Panicked soldiers flee.

Then, without so much as a backward glance, Sorsha flies into the open sky. As she goes, she uses one claw to lash out at the drone filming her. The screen goes dark.

CHAPTER THIRTY-THREE

Alexi comes in alone. "You're awake," he says.

"So it would seem. Where am I?"

"Arcadia."

I pretend to be taking this in. "Valin did this," I say at last, as if I'm putting the pieces together. I let out a bitter laugh that's not entirely faked. "Congratulations. You broke your promise to me, killed my best friend, duped me into almost getting myself killed on the Empty Moon, erased the cousin who betrayed you, tricked me into helping you release a great beast, and now I'm your prisoner. You got everything you wanted."

He shakes his head, more tired than anything else. "This was never what I wanted."

"So what now?" I ask, sitting on the edge of the bed. My hand mere inches away from the hairpins under the pillow. "Dramatic execution? A quick, private death?"

"What about a truce instead?"

I stare at him, profoundly mistrustful. "And what kind of truce would that be?"

He doesn't answer me straight away. His throat moves as he swallows. He goes to the window and looks outside, as if searching for something, and his face softens. "I'll give up my claim to the throne of Kali," he says quietly.

Too stunned to speak, I just goggle at him.

"Elvar can have the throne," he goes on, turning back to me. If there's one thing I've learned, it's that I don't know my brother as well as I once thought I did. Yet his eyes, so wide and so sad, seem sincere. "Max can inherit after him. Bear and I will never make a move to take it back again. All we want in return is for the war and our exile to end. Arcadia will remain our home, but Kali will always be part of us. You know that. We just want to be able to see it again. Mother, too."

The frantic flutter of my heart feels a lot like panic. "I don't believe you."

"Bear and I have talked about it. We could be happy here." His face softens again, the same expression he wore when he looked out the window. "I love the snow. I love the yellow woods and the sun. We have borders with Winter, where we have friends." He gestures around us. "We built this palace. We dreamed up everything Maya Sura created in his illusion and we can make every last bit of it real. We can make this city something special. Arcadia will never be Kali, but I think it could be enough."

"You've spent almost five years trying to take your crown back. Why change your mind now?"

His voice is so soft, I almost don't hear him. "Atonement."

"You're a liar." My temper rises. *Atonement.* No. He can't. Not that. "This isn't about atoning for what you've done. You know you crossed a line when you released Sorsha and you're afraid of what everyone will think of you when they realize what you've really done. So you want to make your move before that happens. You want to be the hero who selflessly gave up his throne to end a terrible war before it could devour the world."

"That's not what this is about," he protests. "You think I imagine myself to be a hero, but I don't."

"Don't you?"

"I used to. I used to believe my talent and my honor made me better than everyone else. But I'm not that boy anymore. I've done so much wrong, Esmae," he says, his voice cracking. "I just want to do something right. I'm not going to pretend I've stopped caring what people think of me, but I swear to you I don't want this truce so I can be the hero who stopped this war. I just want to hate myself a little less."

"And you expect me to believe that?" I demand. "Your word is worth nothing, Alex. You've broken your promises before. Who's to say you wouldn't walk right into the palace on Kali and assassinate Elvar the moment he agreed to this truce and allowed you to set foot on his kingdom?"

"I can't make you believe me." He rakes a hand through his hair, then says, "I don't need your permission, Esmae. You don't rule Kali. Our uncle does. He decides whether or not to end this war, not you. You have no real power."

I stop breathing. I want to tear his face off. I have worked for years to get what he was born to. I have spent my entire life fighting to get all the way across the Warlords board and become a queen. While he showed off in tournaments and shone bright in the sun, I had to claw my way out of the dark and earn every scrap of power I have. And in spite of all that, no matter what I do, there is always someone ready to remind me that I am just a pawn on the board.

You have no real power.

Alex seems to realize he has gone too far. The look of remorse on his face seems genuine, but I hate him too much to care. He takes a step toward me. "Esmae," he says desperately, "There is no way you and I both survive this war. We have to stop before it's too late. *Please*. We can't let this be the way we end."

"What about Rama?" My voice sounds so cold and hollow. "How does his murder fit into your truce?"

A flush burns its way across Alex's face. He can't look me in the eye as he says, "If there's a truce, I would ask that there be no punishment for what happened to Rama."

I can see his mouth moving, but I can't hear him anymore. I can only hear the scream inside my head.

"Your atonement is a lie if you won't atone for that," I tell him.

Then, my fist closing over one of the hairpins, I pounce. I catch him by surprise and my shoulder crashes into his chest, sending us both to the floor. I lash out with my closed fist and feel the *crack* against his jaw. I think it hurts my fist more than it hurts his face. We both scramble back to our feet.

Alexi's posture changes, his entire body realigning itself into a sharp line. I can see the warrior wake up. "Is this really what you want?"

"You were the one who wanted a duel once," I say. "Now we can find out which of us would have won."

There are no swords, but our fight is perhaps what our duel would have been. A step this way, a hand up to block a blow, an elbow to the face, a knee to the groin, duck, spin, hit, hit, *hit* until our fists bleed and our skin is mottled with bruises. And with each strike, each dodge, each thump of my frantic, furious heart, I see Rama dying, Rama twirling me in the ice forest, Rama sprawled across a sofa pretending to be asleep, Rama fading away into the stars. *You have no real power.*

Alex is stronger than I am, but I'm faster than he is. He throws me against a wall and strikes, but I'm gone so fast his bloody fist hits only the stone. *You have no real power. You have no real power. You have no real power.* I snarl like the monster I am and drag my brother to the floor by his shirt. Before he can throw me off, I open my closed fist and press the sharp end of the hairpin to the fluttering vein in his throat.

He goes still at once. We're both breathing hard and fast, our knuckles bleeding, our hair sticky with sweat. My hand trembles, the hairpin thrumming against his skin. All it would take is a small push.

And then we hear a woman's sharp voice:

"Stop!"

CHAPTER THIRTY-FOUR

"Mother."

It slips between my teeth before I can stop it. *Mother.* The word weighs more than the universe to me, but it doesn't move her. She's cold and untouchable as she gazes steadily at me. I've looked into the eyes of wolves, garuda, demons, gods, and monsters, but none have judged me as mercilessly as she does.

Almost eighteen years. That's how long I've spent longing to see my mother, wanting answers even after I realized the truth of what she did to me, and now she's here. And this is how she sees me. Ragged and bleeding, holding a hairpin to her son's throat.

I drop the hairpin and let Alex go. We both stand slowly. My heart races. Our mother stands in the doorway, silent, unmoving. She's like a statue carved out of marble, with soft brown skin, sharp features, long hair knotted loosely on her head, and gray eyes fixed coldly on us both.

"How alike you look," she says, but it doesn't sound like she means it as a compliment.

"We," Alex starts, "I. We."

"Go get yourself cleaned up," she says to him.

He shakes his head, a quick, sharp jerk. "I'm not leaving you alone with her."

That hits me deeper than any of the times his fist met my skin. Does he really think I would hurt our mother?

"Do as you're told, Alexi," our mother replies. "I want to speak to my daughter alone."

My daughter. I shouldn't seize hold of those words and turn them over and over, like a beautiful pebble that catches the light just so, but I do. *My daughter*. "I'll behave," I say, so desperate to be alone with her that I'll say anything.

Alex stays a moment longer, his jaw clenched as he stares at our mother. Then he walks out.

I'm too shy to speak, so I just wait. I lift a hand to smooth down my loose, sweaty curls, then realize how absurd it is to worry about what my mother thinks of my *hair*.

"Come," my mother says after a moment. "Let's go outside."

She walks out of the room without making sure I follow her, but of course I follow her. She leads me down the same hallways and stairs that Max carried me up. We end up in the courtyard, with snow on the cobblestones and an impossible mango tree at the far end. The sun set a little while ago and the courtyard is cold, dark, and silent.

"What would you have done if I hadn't stopped you?" she asks me without looking at me.

I want to lie, I want to *not* be the thing she's been afraid of all my life, but I find myself telling her the truth. "I don't know."

"You know about what happened to your father, I suppose?"

This surprises me, but I nod. I wonder how she lives with the grief of knowing he had been alive for years only to be lost all over again. "I'm sorry."

"Thank you." A polite reply to a polite gesture of sympathy. "I wanted to speak to you alone so I could ask a favor of you." She turns now and the moonlight falls on her face, revealing something I always dreaded seeing. Fear. "Accept the truce Alexi offered you and end this war."

"You're afraid of me."

"No, I am afraid of a curse I know I can't escape." She clasps her hands together. One of them gleams silver in the moonlight. "I am afraid my sons will die."

"One of your sons is a murderer," I say sharply, "and he is so unwilling to make amends for it that one of the conditions of his truce was that there be no punishment for Rama's death."

Her lips press together in a straight line, like she's holding in something she dearly wants to say. "Then is that a no?"

"Yes. He can present his offer to Elvar if he wants, but *I* won't be part of it."

"What if I offer you something you want?"

"What I want is to see Alexi punished for what he did."

"Perhaps there's something you want more." My mother considers me. "You know, you were born first."

"What?"

"No one asked," she says. "When the world found out about you, no one bothered to find out who came first. Everyone assumed it was Alexi. It wasn't. It was you. You are seven minutes older than your brother. You are Cassel's heir. So," she goes on, with a shrug, "if you wish it, *you* could be Queen of Kali. Don't accept the truce. Join us instead. We can take back the kingdom and put you on the throne."

You have no real power. But *that* would be real power, wouldn't it?

"And Elvar?"

"He will either surrender or die fighting."

I know which one he would choose. I shake my head. "How can you ask that of me? They were kind to me. They gave me a home and a place in the world. How can you ask me to betray the only family who have loved me?"

"Your brothers are *my* family. I will do whatever it takes to keep them alive."

And there it is. Something shrivels and dies inside me, something I didn't even know had dared to unfurl: hope.

"So you just want me to abandon my war against Alex," I say. "Truce or alliance, you don't care. You just want me to leave him alone."

"I am offering you what you have always wanted. To be part of our family. To be one of us. You could be Queen of Kali, a lifetime away from the servant you once were. I know we don't have much of a relationship now, but that could be different in a few years. In time, we can learn to trust each other, perhaps even love each other." Her face hardens. "But if you continue down this path, if you keep fighting Alexi, I will never be able to love you. I will never be able to forgive you if you bring him to ruin."

A cold wind blows through the courtyard, rippling through my hair and sending a chill all the way into my bones. My fists clench at my sides.

"It makes no difference to me if I was born first," I tell her. "I don't want to be Queen of Kali. I'm not ashamed that I was once a servant. If you knew me at all, you'd know that. You'd know that a crown could never tempt me away from this war. Alexi is not going to get away with what he did to Rama."

"Alexa, be reasonable."

"My name is Esmae!" I snap. "Alexa died in the deep dark of space almost eighteen years ago." I want to turn around and walk away, but all I can see is a lifetime of hope turning to ash and a twin brother who will always win. And all I can feel is *rage*. "You have been so determined to have only two children, Mother, so I'll make you a promise. By the end of this war, you will have only two children. I just can't promise they'll be the ones you want."

Her face pales. "How can you say that? How can you swear such a thing?"

"Easily. Alexi will have to kill me or I will kill him first."

I'm not sure where I plan to go, because I certainly can't march back into the palace and switch off the shield without anyone noticing me now, but I turn away from her. Before I can take more than a step, her prosthetic right hand closes over my wrist and pulls me back toward her.

The metal is like a clamp. An unbreakable grip. Too late, I remember the way General Khay's cold, strong prosthetic arm tightened around my throat and lifted me into the air. Too late, I hear her voice in my ear. *Expect no mercy from them, Esmae, and show them none in return. And never, ever turn your back on them.*

My mother twists my wrist and I buckle to my knees with a cry that's as much surprise as it is pain.

"What are you—"

Silver shines in the moonlight as she raises a knife with her left hand. She brings it down. My vision goes white with pain.

I bite down on my scream, but a howl slips past my teeth anyway. I look down to see my right thumb on the courtyard stone. It's bloody and torn and jagged white bone peeks out of the flesh.

Shock and pain make me dizzy. It was so quick, so *brutal*. She took the thumb from my right hand. Like Ek Lavya, the tragedy that rippled across almost a hundred years to shape the world we know, I have lost my bowstring thumb. I'll never nock an arrow again. I'll never draw a bow. I'll never make a fist. I'll never hold a sword the same way.

I'll never defeat Alexi.

My mother has made sure of that.

Titania knew. I see that now. She knew that my mother would one day get the better of me. *That* was why she wanted General Khay to train me. She wanted me to learn how to fight my own mother.

I stay on my knees after my mother lets me go, reeling from the pain, clutching my bleeding hand to my chest as blood pools into my lap.

"I would have kept my end of the bargain if you had accepted the truce or if you had agreed to join us, you know," my mother says quietly. "I would have welcomed you into whatever home we end up in. We could have perhaps been happy one day, all of us."

"How could I have been happy?" I scrape out each word. "After what he did?"

She smiles, but it's such a sad, bitter smile. "Do you know why he asked that there be no punishment for that boy's death?" She lowers herself to look me in the eye. There are too many ghosts in my mother's gray eyes. "Because he wasn't the one who killed him."

My voice wobbles. "I don't understand."

"Alexi wanted to win that duel to get *Titania*, but he didn't want to kill you. He knew what the gods had seen and he knew you would be the end of him, but still he refused to do what was necessary. He would never have killed you. So Leila Saka injected Alexi and Bear with a serum the night before the duel, so that they wouldn't wake up until well into the day, and I went to see Amba."

"No," I say, hoping that if I say it enough it'll stop the words from coming. "No."

"I had one boon left," says my mother. "She tried to refuse me, but she could not. I asked her to cloak me so that I would look like Alexi. And because I knew she would warn you, I made her swear never to tell you." Her voice is raw with pain, but she smiles ruefully. "Of course, Amba had already made her plans with your friend. She did not tell me, of course. She let me take Alexi's place in the duel. She let me kill the wrong person. So, you see?" Her eyes are too bright in the moonlight, as if there are tears there she refuses to shed. "It was I who tried to kill you."

Mother. The word weighed more than the universe to me . . . and weighed nothing at all to her.

"I didn't want it to come to that," she says, as if that makes it better. "But it was *my* curse. *My* choices. So it was *my* responsibility to protect them from the consequences."

"Shloka?" I croak.

She nods. "Yes. I told Leila to go after you. Alexi and Bear didn't know about that."

"But they knew about the duel. Why didn't they tell me the truth? Why didn't they ever say?"

"Why do you think? They wanted to keep me safe from you. I am not helpless, but I am no match for you either. They believed Alexi stood a better chance at fending off your fury than I did." She stands. "I think it was also a matter of pride. Alexi didn't want to be seen as a coward who sent his mother to do his dirty work."

The world swims in and out. The deception and the betrayal swallow me whole. All this time, it was her. All this time, they lied. Even Bear. For her, for pride, for the family that will never include me. Alex broke his promise to me, tricked me, unleashed beasts to fight me, fought a war for a crown that it turns out was never even his, but he didn't try to murder me on the day of the duel. He didn't murder Rama. Our mother did.

I'm not leaving you alone with her, he said just now. Not because he thought I would hurt her, but because he thought *she* would hurt *me*. And then he left anyway. *He chose her over you, Esmae. There was never a family for you to find with them. They could never have been yours.*

I want to scream, but when I open my mouth, a laugh comes out instead. It's sharp and jagged like glass.

"You should have done a better job," I tell her. "Trying and failing to kill me once is one thing, but trying and failing *three* times seems an awful lot like incompetence. And what about tonight? You could have killed me, but you did this instead?" I hold up my right hand, the four lonely fingers pointing straight up. "Do you really think this will stop me? Do you really think all I am is a bow and a sword? I am more like you than you know, Mother. I will find another way to tear you all apart. *You should have killed me.*"

Blood trickles down my wrist. She stares down at me for a long time, pale and cold and haunted by a ghost I can't see.

Then she reaches out with her prosthetic hand and strokes my hair. I feel it trembling against me. "You're right," she says softly, her eyes still too bright. "You are so much like me."

And then, still stroking my hair, she raises her knife again and glides it gently across my throat.

CHAPTER THIRTY-FIVE

The knife stops halfway across my throat. At first, I think wildly that *she* stopped, that my mother couldn't bring herself to complete what she had started. Then, blinking through the blood and pain, I see that there's another hand on hers.

"Kyra," says Amba, stern and cold, "put the knife down."

My mother makes a sound that's more sob than laugh. "How long have you been watching?"

"I have been here the whole time. A myna in a mango tree. You should have paid more attention. Did you think I wouldn't be close? Did you think for one moment that I, who know exactly what you've done, would leave you alone with your daughter?" Amba's eyes glitter. "You have no boons left, Kyra. Put the knife down or I will make you."

"You can't do that," says my mother. "You can't stop me. You know what it will cost you."

Amba's grip tightens over the knife. "Yes, I do know."

I can't move. I don't dare with the knife still at my throat, blood all over it.

My pulse flutters wildly and I try to speak, but only blood bubbles out of my mouth. I try again. "Amba. Don't. *Don't.*"

"Consider this very carefully, Amba," my mother says. "Is she worth it?"

"The knife. Now."

I know how this is going to go and there is nothing I can do to stop it. My mother is steel itself and she doesn't back down. She wrestles the knife out of Amba's grip and tries to thrust it deeper. Amba slams her palm into the middle of my mother's chest. My mother's eyes widen in shock before she vanishes, knife and all.

Amba sinks to her knees in front of me and presses her forehead to mine. "Forgive me," she whispers, "For all of it."

For just one moment, she smiles at me.

Then she starts to scream.

And there's a roar, from somewhere deep inside the world, a cry of terror and agony that makes my bones tremble.

It's the sound of a god falling.

CHAPTER THIRTY-SIX

Titania

The roar shakes the universe. Everyone hears it. Mortals on every ship and every planet cover their ears and try in vain to block the sound out. They are afraid. They don't understand. Rickard is the only one old enough to remember the last time.

The celestial world knows. They do not all know what has happened or whom it has happened to, but they know what that roar means.

And so, spread far across the galaxy in their temples and their palaces and their realms in the stars, the gods weep.

On the Empty Moon, Vahana raises their head and shrieks into the sky.

Miles ahead of me, as I chase her through the stars, Sorsha howls back into the void.

As for Kirrin, he knows what is about to happen an instant before it does. I see through his eyes, at the gates of Arcadia with Alexi and Bear, when Kyra appears out of nowhere with a bloody knife in her hand and tears in her eyes.

"Kyra," he croaks, "What have you done?"

For he knows there's only one way she could have been sent there like that, and what that would have done to the god who sent her.

There is one other mortal who knows what the roar means, better than anyone else alive. Max is still on his way back to Kali when it happens. The moment he hears the universe scream, he turns his ship around.

I see the blood through Amba's eyes. I see Kyra's knife. I see the desperate hurt in Esmae's face. I feel Amba's pain as she falls.

I spin away from Sorsha and fly to Arcadia.

I should have told Esmae the truth about how Rama died. Maybe she would have seen the knife coming if I had.

I wanted so badly to keep the truth from destroying her, but it came for her and swallowed her up anyway.

CHAPTER THIRTY-SEVEN

This is not supposed to happen to gods. They live while we fade and die. They go on. They're not supposed to fall like Valin did. *But then that's what gods do, isn't it?* I said bitterly to Amba not long ago. *You stand above the rest of us and let us bear the wounds you don't dare risk yourselves.*

She's not standing above me now.

"Amba," I croak, blood sputtering from my throat and mouth as I try to speak.

She's stopped screaming. She sits back on her heels, her shoulders bowed, her brown skin glossy with sweat, her eyes wide and dark. She trembles, but her mouth twists in a what I imagine she thinks is a smile. "Hush," she says, and the tremor in her voice gives away the pain and fear she's trying so desperately to hide. "You'll bleed out if you keep speaking."

She's right. I'm no use to her or to anyone else if I die here. Keeping the four fingers of my right hand pressed against my throat, I fumble in the slick blood and sweat for the bottom of my tunic. I curl my fingers into the fabric and rip off a strip of the cloth. My breath comes out in faint gasps, each one bringing up another spatter of blood. I wrap the torn strip of my tunic around my throat and knot it awkwardly with my left hand to keep it in place. Then I do the same to my right hand with a second piece. It's not much, but it should keep me from bleeding out for a few minutes.

"Good," says Amba. "Good."

I kneel beside her and take her hand. She stays very straight for a moment longer, then her shoulders crumple and she leans on me.

"I'm afraid, Esmae."

"Of what?"

"Of a universe without the stars. Without the celestial realms, without flight, without stardust and godfire. I don't know if I can bear the agony of losing my world."

My cheeks are wet, and I rub the tears away with the back of my wounded hand. "Do you want me to tell you a story?"

"I know all the stories," she replies with some of her old bite.

"You don't know this one."

"Very well," says Amba, "Tell me. In as few words as possible, mind, because I do not think it at all wise to be so chatty with a partly slit throat."

"There was once a little girl who wanted her mother," I whisper. "For years and years, she searched the world. She refused to give up. She fought everyone who tried to stop her, from princes to kings to the gods themselves. Always, always, there was that word driving her on. *Mother*. Like a battle cry, like a favorite song. *Mother*."

"I know this story," Amba says quietly. "I know what happens when she finds her mother in the end."

"That's not the end."

"No?"

"In the end," I tell her, "the little girl, now almost grown, came to see something she had failed to understand before. She saw that all her life, when she called for her mother and thought no one ever answered, someone did. Someone always answered."

Amba doesn't speak, but I don't need her to. I know she understands.

"I love you," I tell her.

She smiles. It's small and trembles on her lips, but it's real. "And I you."

An engine rumbles in the distance. We look up and see a starship slip out of the night sky, landing roughly on the other side of the courtyard wall. A moment later, Max appears over the wall and drops into the courtyard. He staggers briefly to a stop when he sees us and then rushes the rest of the way.

"Your throat," he says hoarsely. "You should be dead."

"It is thanks to yours truly that she isn't, second favorite brother of mine," says Amba.

"Who's your favorite?" he asks her, putting his fingers to the pulse on the inside of my wrist.

"Tyre, obviously. He never causes me any trouble." Amba frowns. "Max, you're kneeling on Esmae's severed thumb."

He gives the stone beneath him a startled look and swears under his breath.

"That's not very kind of you, Max," I say mournfully. "I think my thumb has suffered enough tonight, don't you?"

"*Tyre* would never have been so cruel to Esmae's thumb," Amba chimes in.

Max ignores our nonsense and rather sensibly attends to practical matters instead. He fishes a medical laser out of the pocket of his jacket. He reaches for the bloody strip of cloth around my throat. "I'm taking this off, okay? I need to seal the wound up before you bleed right out."

I tense as the cloth comes off, pulling bits of dried blood with it. Max immediately switches the laser on and slides the hot beam of light over the gash in my throat. It hurts like all hell, but I have to admit it's not as bad as having my shoulder stitched up by hand. When Max draws back, there's only a dull ache and a knotted scar where the wound was.

Then he works on the open wound where my severed thumb was. He's precise and gentle, his hands as steady as they are when he paints wooden carousels and creates birds out of feathers and metal. I've often thought he's so much better at fixing things than he is at breaking them.

I'm the opposite.

"Do you want me to call him?" Max asks Amba.

"I suppose you had better."

Max finishes sealing my hand. Then he calls for Kirrin.

Kirrin appears at once. He's frantic. "I couldn't find you," he says to Amba, his entire body shaking as he kneels beside her. "I couldn't find you."

She puts her hand over his. "I have been severed from the celestial world. You won't be able to feel me anymore."

I look at them side by side and marvel at how brightly Kirrin shines. The blue of his skin glows like moonlight. I was always so used to Amba that I never realized she used to shine like that, too. Now she's almost gray, with only the faintest glimmer of otherworldly light left on her mortal skin.

"Kirrin, you know what to do," says Max. "Quickly, before the last of the stardust fades."

Kirrin bows his head and presses his hands together. He closes his eyes and his mouth moves quickly and silently as if in prayer. When he opens his eyes, there's a golden dagger in his cupped hands.

"Take it," he says to Amba, "Like Valin did. When you fell, you were cursed to live a mortal life, but you needn't live it like this. You can be reborn with no memory of what you once were. You can have love, friendship, and family. A life where you won't ever miss the stars."

She puts her hand on the hilt of the dagger. I swallow hard. *Don't go*, I want to say. *Please don't leave me*.

"Take it," I say instead. "Go while you can."

Amba gives me a long look, then slowly moves her hand away. "No," she says to Kirrin. "I cannot go."

"Amba, you can't be serious," Kirrin protests. "You can't exactly change your mind next week! Once the last of the stardust in your skin fades, you won't be able to use the dagger. You know that. You know you're running out of time!"

"Everyone feels the need to tell me about the consequences of my choices as if I am not entirely aware of them already," she snaps at him, "And I am frankly tired of it. Put the dagger away, Kirrin. I will not be using it." She sighs, looks at both of her brothers' faces, and then says more gently, "This is not like when Valin fell. I cannot just go in peace. I have done too much harm to leave before I have a chance to put it right. I have too much to make amends for, too much still to see and too much life left to live."

Kirrin and I glance at each other, on the same side for once. Neither of us wants her to go, but we both know she'll never be whole without the stars if she stays.

But Max, who knows how she feels better than either of us, doesn't argue with her. Still holding my hand, his white knuckles the only sign of his grief, he looks his sister in the eye and says only, "Are you sure?"

"I am."

"Then that's that," he says.

Kirrin closes his fists and the golden dagger disappears.

"One day they will both be gone for good," he says. "And I will never see either of them ever again."

Amba and Max don't react to this at all, and I realize belatedly that only I could hear him. It was a lament he needed to give voice to, but he didn't want to burden them with it. I give him a slight nod, the only way I can show him I heard him. I understood.

"Let's get into the ship," says Max. "We can't stay here."

"I'll keep everyone away from the palace until you're gone," says Kirrin. "It's the least I can do."

He vanishes.

I stand up carefully and let go of Max's hand. I'm unsteady on my feet, probably from blood loss and shock, but I take a few shaky steps to the mango tree and suck in a few breaths of cold, sharp air.

As they make their way to the wall, I hear Max ask Amba, almost conversationally, "So where are you going to live now that you have a mortal life ahead of you?"

"You're a crown prince with a palace, aren't you?" Amba replies. "Do you not have a suitably luxurious room for me?"

"It's customary in the mortal world to wait for an invitation."

"An invitation? Need I remind you of the time I killed our father to save your life?"

"I was wondering when that would come up," says Max. "It's been at least an hour since you last mentioned it."

"That is an outrageous exaggeration!"

Their voices fade in and out, almost in time with the throb of my hand. I look down at the pale scar. It feels like every horror is in that scar. The gaping wound where my thumb should be. My brother's betrayal. My mother's secrets. Rama's death. Amba's fall. A teacher, a betrayal, a king, an arrow, a crown, a spaceship, a curse, a queen, a wish, a flower, a knife. A cycle that never, ever ends.

I am more like you than you know, Mother.

In the sky, I see a glimmer of light that I know so well. A small smile lifts the corner of my mouth.

"Go without me," I say.

Max and Amba both stop in their tracks. "No," they say at the same time.

"You heard what he said," I say, deliberately not saying Kirrin's name in case it gets his attention. "He's keeping everyone away. This is my chance to go back into the palace and find the generator without anyone interfering."

Amba, ever the war goddess, cocks her head. "That's actually an excellent strategy," she says.

"It is, but it's more important that we get out of here," says Max. "We don't know how long he'll be able to keep Alex away."

I shake my head. "I came here to deactivate the shield. If I leave without doing that, it'll be because my mother broke me. I can't let her have that."

"Then we'll wait for you in the ship."

"No. I'll follow you. I promise. Look." I point up into the sky. "That's *Titania*. She's coming. I'll get out of here with her, but I need you both to get out of Arcadia now. Please."

"Why?"

I look at him, into those dark eyes that have always seen me. "You know why." And he does. I can see he does.

He's quiet for a moment and then he lets out a sharp breath. He reaches up to his ear, pulls out his earpiece, and hands it to me. "You'll need a way to talk to *Titania*." I had to give mine up before we got here. Our ruse wouldn't have worked if Kirrin had seen it. "Esmae—"

"I know," I say quickly. I don't think I can bear to hear it right now. "Me too."

I watch them go over the wall. Then I turn back to the palace.

CHAPTER THIRTY-EIGHT

My brother's palace is eerily quiet when I go back inside. I stay very still and listen. Beyond the silence, beyond the sound of the wind outside, I can hear *something*.

It's the hum of a generator.

I track the sound until I reach a set of steps leading down into what is most likely some kind of cellar. Before I head down to take a closer look, I double back to a window to make sure Max's ship actually takes off. My chest loosens a little as I watch it vanish into the sky. They're safe.

At the bottom of the steps is a kitchen. Clean, a little chaotic. Pots, pans, and dough on the counters, like dinner is under way.

There's also a maid standing by the counter with a rolling pin. She stares at me in horror. I can only imagine what I must look like.

"Where is everyone?"

"It's just me on duty tonight," she squeaks, her wide eyes darting past me as if she's wondering if she stands any chance at fleeing. I don't blame her. With all the blood on me, I probably look like I've killed half a dozen people.

I step aside. "The princes are at the city gates. You'd better go tell them their sister is in the palace."

She doesn't need telling twice. She drops the rolling pin and runs. Good. She'll be outside the gates by the time I'm done.

There's no sign of the generator in the kitchen, but I can still hear it. There's a locked door on the other side of the room. I break the lock with the discarded rolling pin and pull open the door.

The generator is little more than a metal box on a table, with a single green light and a screen split into several windows, each showing me footage in real time of how the illusion looks from outside the shield. Just as Maya Sura said, there's nothing fancy about this generator. My brother didn't bother to protect it because he never expected an enemy to get close to it.

The rolling pin is still in my left hand. I stare at it for a moment, at my left hand where I should be seeing my right. Then I activate the earpiece Max gave me.

"Esmae!" *Titania* sounds frantic as her voice crackles to life over my earpiece. "There you are! Are you okay?"

"Are you?" I ask. "Is Sybilla safe?"

"Yes, we're fine. She's here with me. We were chasing Sorsha, but we came back when Amba fell. I think the helmet has lost all hold on her, Esmae. I don't think it's going to be long before she starts devouring stars."

And with Amba now mortal, there's no way to take Sorsha back to Anga and reactivate the helmet.

"Esmae, if she starts eating the stars—"

She doesn't need to finish. I know. If Sorsha starts devouring the stars, it will only be a matter of time before she swallows our sun.

After a moment of silence, *Titania* speaks again. "We just passed Max's ship. He says you're still in the palace. Where do you want us to meet you?"

"Are you cloaked?"

"Of course."

"Then hover right above the shield. I need you to tell me if this works."

I tighten my grip on the rolling pin once again and smash the generator to pieces. It's unnecessarily violent, but the hurt needs somewhere to go. As the screen shatters and goes dark, I catch a glimpse of the green light. It's red now.

"The shield is down!" *Titania* crows in my ear. "You did it! I did it! We all did it!" In the background, I can hear Sybilla whooping. "Come to top of the tower and we'll pick you up. You need to get out of there!"

I don't say anything.

"Esmae?"

"What's going on at the gates?" I ask her, making my way back up the kitchen steps. It's a few twists and turns from there to the palace doors. "Can you see?"

"Chaos," says *Titania*, with a certain gleeful satisfaction. "There was already some unrest after Sorsha took off, but now the formations have completely broken. Soldiers are spilling past the gates and spreading out into the city. I suspect Alexi's allies have had something of a shock and are now trying to see for themselves if the city that just vanished before their eyes is really gone."

I step out of the palace. Far away, beyond the palace wall and the wood piles and unfinished rooftops, I see dark specks moving against the white snow. Soldiers, just like she said.

I move in the opposite direction. Some distance behind the palace is the forest of yellow trees that stretch all the way out of the city. With the shield down, that's my best way out. The trees will give me some cover.

"Why are you outside?" *Titania* demands. Her tone has sharpened. I look back at the sky above the palace, but she's still cloaked so I can't see her. "Where are you going? Why aren't you coming to the top of the tower?"

"I can't," I say softly. "I've lost too much blood to make it up all those stairs."

"Then we'll come down there and pick you up."

"No. Not yet." I close my eyes for a moment. "I need you to do something for me."

"Anything," she says at once.

I am more like you than you know, Mother.

We could be happy here.

You have no real power.

You are so much like me.

We can make this city something special. Arcadia will never be Kali, but I think it could be enough.

We could be happy here.

The last time I trained with General Khay, I told her I never stop screaming.

And you never will, she said, *not until you can let them go. You are not ready to hear this, Esmae, but one day you will be.*

Again and again, I have been told to let them go. I never did. I never could. And this is where it led me.

247

We could be happy here.

I have been screaming since Rama died and I think, at long last, it's time to stop.

"Turn Arcadia to ash," I say to *Titania*.

There is total silence for an instant and then I hear her shock. "The sun has gone down," she protests. "And there are soldiers all over the city now. I can't use my weapons against them. The laws of righteous warfare—"

"I don't care about the laws of righteous warfare."

"I do! You know what I am, Esmae. You know what I'm capable of. I'm a monster without those laws!"

"No," I remind her gently. "Never. You're the arrow, remember? I'm the archer."

The woods are only about a hundred feet ahead of me when *Titania* speaks. "All of Arcadia?"

"Leave my brothers and mother. Let them watch. Destroy the rest, from the gates to the edge of the yellow woods, every tile, every rock, every brick. Burn it all down."

"What about you?"

"I'll get to the woods." I stumble on.

"I'm the arrow," she says.

"And I'm the archer."

There's a ripple in the sky as *Titania* deactivates her cloaking system and flickers into sight. I hear the shouts of soldiers as they see her. I even think, though it's not possible from this far away, that I hear the sound of her five launchers clicking into place. Righteousness, Strength, Courage, Beauty, and Patience. They have never all been used at the same time before.

"Run faster, Esmae," *Titania* says.

So I run. And the world behind me explodes in white fire.

CHAPTER THIRTY-NINE

Titania

As ash settles quietly on the snow where Arcadia once was, the whole world watches. Until something even more terrible eclipses what we have done.

In the sky, stars go out.

Acknowledgements

This was an incredibly hard book to write. Maybe it was because of how much pain Esmae is in, which only too closely mirrors my own depression. Maybe it was because I knew how many people loved the first book and couldn't bear to let them down. Or maybe it was a harder book because some books just *are*.

Whatever the reason, writing this book wouldn't have been possible without the support of so many people. To my husband Steve, above all else, who never stops believing in me and who makes sure I have the time and space to disappear behind my laptop for as long as necessary. To Jem, Henry, and Juno, who may sometimes kick off when I have to leave them to get the words written, but who always forgive me. To my parents, who read this mere hours after I finished writing it and categorically assured me that it was not terrible. To my brother, who has a cute dog.

To Eric Smith, who believed in this story before anyone else in publishing did. To Penny Moore, who carves new paths for me. To Alison Weiss, who fights so fiercely for me and for my books. To Nicole Frail, for pointing out all the ways this book shines and showing me how it can shine brighter. To Kate Gartner, Johanna Dickson, and the rest of the team at Skyhorse, for the gorgeous covers, interiors, and endless support.

To Amina, Nipsi, Lindsey, Katy, and Gemma, who keep me firmly on the ground when I wander off into the clouds. To Sue, Anne, and Grace, for years of pretending to be interested when I talk about my books. And to the wonderful authors who make this journey seem so much less lonely: Natasha, Samira, Kati, Elsie, and so, so many others. Thank you. Thank you for every 2 a.m. tweet, every three-hour chat, every bit of gossip, every laugh, every time you saw me struggling and said, "You can do this."

To the bloggers who put their heart and soul into books and into this community, and especially to Shealea for all the support, enthusiasm, and for so passionately shouting to the world about *A Spark of White Fire* over the past year.

And finally, to you. To the readers. Know that every time you send me a message to say you loved my book, every time you mention my books on your list of favorites, every time you write a review or tag me in a post or send me an email just to say hi, you make every moment I spend writing these stories worth it. Thank you.